BIGFOOT RIDGE

Bigfoot Ridge

by

C.E. Osborn

This is a work of fiction. Names, characters, businesses, places, events and incidents are either the products of the author's imagination or used in a fictitious manner. Any resemblance to actual persons, living or dead, or actual events is purely coincidental.

Cover design:
SelfPubBookCovers.com/Viergacht

© 2024
C.E. Osborn
All rights reserved

For Jennifer R.

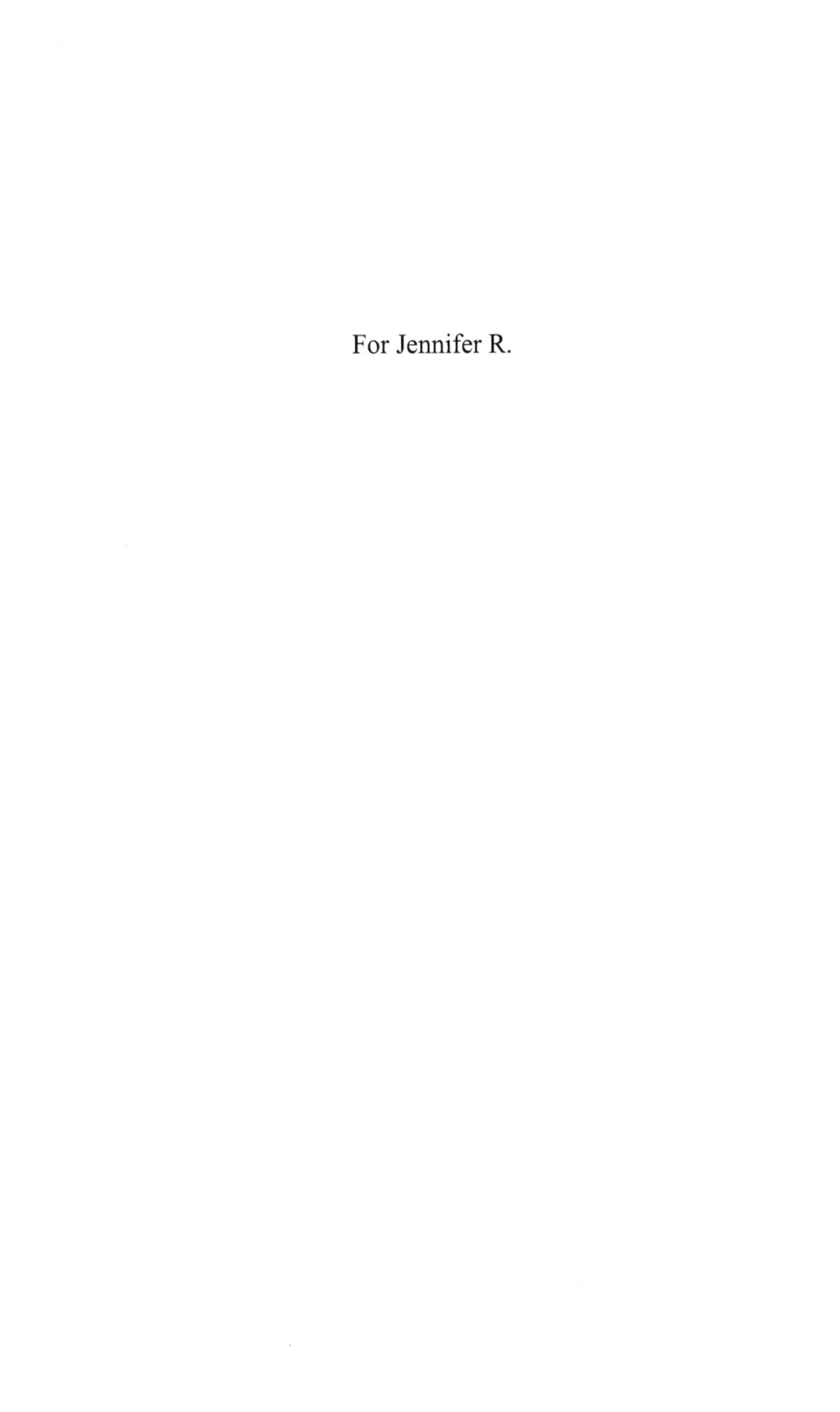

CHAPTER 1

Autumn Hunter opened the front door to her house, entered the hallway, dropped her handbag carelessly on a side table, and closed the door behind her. Automatically making sure it was locked, she shook her head and turned left into the living room. Her cat, Squatch, sat up from his usual sleeping place on the couch and studied her as she sank onto a cushion next to him. She reached out to pet him and her eyes wandered around the room.

"Two weeks of furlough," she said out loud. That was the news she, and employees in every department at the public library system, had received today. To save some money in the budget, they were all being placed on brief furloughs, in varied schedules so the library could still function. Autumn had been one of the people chosen to go on leave first.

"I have the next two weeks off, unpaid," she told the cat. He blinked and jumped off the couch, heading for his empty bowl in the kitchen. "What am I going to do?"

For a couple of minutes, she contemplated calling her boyfriend, Zach Larson, and asking if she could come visit him. It was early October, and he had been gone for a couple of weeks. He was currently somewhere else in the country, filming for the reality television show *Creature Hunt*. She stood and went over to the computer, where he had left a calendar of expected locations and dates. She looked at the calendar for today's date and saw that he was currently in New Jersey. The show had decided to revisit some locations this season, and he and his crew were on the hunt for a possible sighting of the Jersey Devil in the Pine Barrens.

It had been Autumn's intense interest in Bigfoot, and the show, that had led to her meeting Zach a couple of years ago. They had moved in together last year, and she was used to his absence by now. She thought again about trying to plan a visit. Deep down, she knew it wouldn't be a great idea. He would be busy following leads and interviewing witnesses, and even though she might be able to help with parts of the investigation, she would probably be more of a distraction than he needed while on camera.

She did want to hear his voice, though, and retrieved her cell phone from her bag. She walked to the kitchen to feed Squatch, then dialed Zach's number and sat down in front of the computer. She automatically went to the website of the Bigfoot Online Group, or BOG. She and several of her friends often went on local hunts for Bigfoot. Maybe there had been some interesting leads and sightings somewhere in the state in recent weeks.

"Hi, Autumn." Zach's warm voice instantly made her feel better. "How are you?"

"It hasn't been a great day," she said. She explained about the furlough. "I have two weeks off. For which I'm not getting paid. Any suggestions?"

"I think we're okay on the financial end," he said. "We've both got money saved for something like this. What about getting some work done on the book?"

Autumn sighed. "I've been trying to work on ideas for different chapters every night for the last month, since we got back from Tahoma Valley. I haven't gotten very far." She and Zach had committed themselves to writing a book on cryptozoology and looking for creatures that were commonly called monsters. The project had been going on for several months, but there were times that Autumn had found it difficult to concentrate on the actual writing. She much preferred being out in the field.

"I wish I could fly you out here, but today is our last day in New Jersey. Then we're going to Arkansas."

"The Boggy Creek monster?" Autumn sat up. She had several books about the legendary Bigfoot-type creature on her bookshelf.

"Yep. A return from an episode we did back in the first season. Hold on a minute." She heard him cover the phone and talk to someone in the background. "Hey, Brandon's here. We're about ready to head out into the Pine Barrens."

"Be careful," she warned.

"I always try to be careful. Look, if you're feeling restless, why not call up some of your friends? Weren't Nate and Mike going out to the Olympic Peninsula around now? Maybe you can take a vacation."

"Sure," she said. She started scrolling down the BOG forum. "Maybe I'll do that."

"Great. I'll talk to you soon. Love you, Autumn."

"Love you too, Zach."

She chuckled when she hung up the phone. Their conversations often led to suggestions of looking for monsters. Her eyes stopped on the words "Olympic National Park" and "Bobcat Lake" as she scanned the page in front of her. She clicked into the message and realized that she may have found something to occupy her time for at least several days.

"Footprints near Marmot Trail. Probably twenty inches long!" she read out loud. "Felt I was being watched when I found them." She checked the date on the post. It had been added to the forum this morning.

Her next action was to call her friend Mike. He and her other longtime friend, Nate, worked in IT, and their jobs frequently let them work from home. They also had a lot of paid time off at their job, and earlier in the month they had indeed mentioned that they were planning to head out to Bobcat Lake for a long weekend. She smiled when Mike answered the phone. "Hi, Autumn. Let me guess. You read the BOG forum and want us to go on a Bigfoot hunt."

"Hello," she laughed. "You're not too far off. I've been placed on a furlough for two weeks, and Zach is out of town.

I did see some mention of footprint sightings around a place called Marmot Trail. Is that close to the lake?"

"I'm not sure. We got here yesterday and haven't strayed too far from the resort. You happened to catch us in a good cell reception area right now, though. We're in Port Mason, doing some shopping. The cabins we're staying in have spotty cell service and internet, but they're very nice. There's also a lodge and an onsite restaurant."

"Of course. Where are these wondrous accommodations?"

"Bobcat Lodge, right off of Highway 101 on the lake. Are you coming up? We have a two-bedroom cabin with a loft. Nate and Tiffany are in one bedroom with a king-size bed. I'm currently in the other bedroom, but I can move up to the loft. It's got a twin bed and a privacy curtain with a half bath."

"Actually, the loft sounds perfect for me," she assured him. "I can drive up tomorrow, if that's okay. I'll probably arrive mid-afternoon."

"Great. I'll let Nate and Tiffany know."

Autumn ended the call and texted Erica to see if she'd be able to take time off. Her friend reminded her that she had just started a new job, but she hoped Autumn had fun and stayed safe in the forest. The other member of their group, Bill, who was Mike's cousin, was also currently busy with work. Autumn finally put down the phone and wandered into the kitchen. As happened quite frequently when Zach was away, she decided to order dinner. While waiting for her food, she started to pack for her trip to Bobcat Lake. She was excited about going out on another Bigfoot investigation.

Jenna Stalberg picked up her drink and sipped while she looked in the direction of the sunset. When she and her husband Donnie had met with the previous owners to talk about the sale of the resort, they had sat right here on the deck behind the main lodge, right around this time of day.

The sunset was brilliant and waves of color spread out from behind the mountains just to the southwest of Bobcat Lake.

"Mojito again?" Donnie asked, coming up behind her and placing his hand on her shoulders. He had slid out the back door from the restaurant, where he managed the staff and kept an eye on the diners. It was just past the busiest time for dinner, and several guests were walking past them on their way back to their cabins.

"Of course," she said. "Have a seat, dear."

He sat down next to her and smiled, holding up a bottle of beer in a salute. "Here's to a great first season at Bobcat Lodge."

"And to many more," she replied, clinking her glass against the bottle.

They had bought the resort almost a year ago from a couple anxious to sell the property. Jenna had been an office project manager, while Donnie had kept busy for several years as a corporate human resources employee, a restaurant manager, and a backup singer for a few local bands. They were both from Port Mason, just thirty minutes away, and their twenty-five-year-old daughter Sarah now occupied the house they had left behind in town.

Bobcat Lodge consisted of a central lodge building, three stories tall and built out of wood. It had maintained the log cabin façade over the years, but several renovations and additions had necessitated that the inside of the building was completely modern. There were twenty-seven guest rooms in the lodge, and ten cabins that varied from small studios to two-bedroom luxury accommodations. A restaurant, coffee bar, gift shop, and rooms for guest computer use, a library with books and games, and a small medical center completed the lodge interior. Jenna and Donnie also had their own private apartment on the first floor, overlooking the lake.

"I see Laine Dawson and Cole Patterson are here for a few days," Donnie said. "Cole mentioned that he had talked to another group of people up here that might be looking for Bigfoot."

Jenna laughed. "Yep. That group in Cabin Ten. One of the guys mentioned a friend of theirs was driving up for a few days. She's checking in tomorrow."

"You think they're going to find anything?"

"No," Jenna said. "Despite the fact that Cole really seems to think that we somehow have our own private monster here on the property, I don't think anyone looking for Bigfoot or any other monster is going to see one while they're here."

"Oh, that flying thing he keeps claiming he saw? What'd he call it? Batman, or something?"

"Batsquatch, dear."

"Oh, right." Donnie looked at the lake. "Did Jake come by here this morning?"

"He always does. He's stopped checking on the caretaker's cabin, though." Ranger Jake Tyler had made the resort a regular stop on his patrol since they had opened to the public in April. The former caretaker's cabin had been where his father had lived for a couple of years, before the fire that had closed down the property three years ago. Tate Tyler had died in the fire. Jake often walked down the trail where the cabin was located, abandoned since that night, just to check on the damaged building.

"Good. Time to move on."

"Hey, did you hear something howling last night?" Jenna asked. She had been woken up in the night by a long, almost mournful sound. It had sounded like a wolf, at least to her inexperienced ears, which was impossible. There were no wolves known to be living in Olympic National Park.

"Nope. Dead asleep." Donnie finished his beer and checked his watch. "Time to start closing things down."

"I'll check on the reception desk in a few minutes," Jenna said. Donnie went back into the building, and Jenna saw Laine and Cole walking in the direction of the parking lot, a duffel bag in Cole's hand. She frowned and wondered what they were up to. She really liked Laine, but thought that Cole was way too obsessed with strange creatures for his own good.

She finished her drink and carried the glass with her into the building, leaving it in the sink in the kitchen. Making her way around the busy staff members, she emerged into the lobby to make sure the evening receptionist had arrived and all the paperwork was in order. With that taken care of, she went to their apartment and closed the door, shutting out the bustle of the resort. While she loved her job, she also loved the fact that she had her own private retreat here on site to get away from the demands of the guests. "Monsters," she said as she sank into her favorite recliner. "No one's going to find any monsters here."

CHAPTER 2

Ranger Jake Tyler turned off his computer and sighed, unable to believe the question he had just been asked on the phone. After five years as a National Park Service Ranger, he was still surprised by the most basic questions that he heard from the public when he was out on patrol. "No, you shouldn't bring steak along to feed a bear," he heard himself saying to an eager-sounding man on the other end of the phone. "Be sure you have bear spray with you, and make sure you're making noise on the trail so they stay away."

He hung up and the man standing in the doorway of the small office crossed his arms and grinned. "Glad it's closing time, Jake?" Aaron Washington asked.

"Yes, Aaron. I'm very happy that it's closing time." Jake mustered a smile for his co-worker. Jake got up from his desk, walked down the hall, and passed the displays and book shelves in the main room, only pausing for a few seconds to make sure everything was in place. The only vehicles visible in the parking lot were two park service vehicles, Aaron's sedan, and Jake's truck.

Aaron was one of several park rangers who rotated to different stations within the park and greeted visitors coming to get permits, check weather conditions, and browse the natural history information available at each location. Jake was a law enforcement ranger, and this was his permanent station. He had requested it from the start, mostly to keep an eye on a particular area down the road that seemed to attract people thinking they could get a glimpse of the state's most legendary creature, Bigfoot.

Most of the people he encountered trying to get into that property were decent folks who really just wanted an excuse to go out for a hike, but claimed the Marmot Trail, just down the road, had felt too crowded. He tried to steer them to other places around Bobcat Lake, reminding them to stop by the station to let a ranger know they were going to be on a particular trail. Those people often made him smile, because they were usually easy to deal with once they realized that the area had been set aside for scientific and natural research. Most of them never questioned what kind of research, or why there was a locked metal gate keeping people away from that part of the forest.

Then there were people like the man he had encountered earlier in the day while on one of his routine patrols around the lake. Cole Patterson was well-known to law enforcement in the park, as he had been caught more than once disturbing the people living along the lake, trying to ask them questions about strange animals or creatures he had heard about somewhere else. It was a quiet, peaceful neighborhood down there, the families had all passed down the cabins for a couple of generations, and despite the stories they had shared with Jake, they didn't like being questioned about monsters in the woods surrounding their homes.

Jake lived among them, in a cabin once occupied by his parents, and had seen Cole and his girlfriend, Laine Dawson, sneaking past a couple of cabins to get to the lake shore. Cole had been talking about unusual prints, and Laine had been keeping an eye out for anyone approaching them. When Jake had identified himself, Cole had insisted that the residents knew that something large and unknown was creeping around the cabins.

Jake knew Cole was correct about the other residents keeping a secret, but he respected his neighbors. That had been back in May, and to Laine's credit she had insisted to Cole that they leave. Since then, Cole seemed to be obeying Jake's orders to go do his monster hunting somewhere else.

"I'm heading out," Aaron said, jolting Jake from his thoughts. "See you tomorrow."

"Bye." Jake watched Aaron until the other ranger went to his car, then headed back to his office. He had one place to check before heading home.

A picture of his father on his desk gave him pause as he was putting on his jacket. Tate Tyler had been a park ranger for thirty years in the Olympic National Park before retiring several years ago. After Jake's mother died, his father had been offered a job as a caretaker at Bobcat Lodge, a resort on the opposite shore of the lake.

Jake had visited his father at the small, yet comfortable, cabin he had been given as part of the job, set back from the guest cabins in the forest and only accessible from one of the walking trails on the property. Each time he had walked on that trail, he had felt that something was watching him, and the silence that often fell over the area was eerie. Tate had shrugged it off. "There's no animal out here that I haven't encountered before," he had said. Even though Jake disagreed, he had dropped the issue. Even when there were sounds in the woods, howling and occasional unusual calls that couldn't be explained, Tate had refused to believe that anything was wrong.

One night three years ago, he had received a call saying that there had been a fire at the resort and his father was missing. He had driven over in a daze, following another ranger's truck through the property and down the path that was thankfully wide enough for rescue vehicles. He had waited by his truck during the search, and it had not taken long for two other rangers to discover Tate's body.

Tate's wounds didn't appear to have been caused by a fire, as there were very few signs of burns on his skin. He was determined to have died from blood loss and shock from a traumatic blow. Tate had met with a powerful force that hit him hard enough to crush part of his skull. A large branch had been found nearby, covered with blood. The gaping wound had caused the quick death, Jake had been told.

Standing near his father's body, Jake had noticed that the end of the tree limb was not cut, as initially thought, but was splintered, as if it had been torn off one of the nearby trees. He had returned to the cabin while medical personnel had taken over. Standing just outside the partly burned structure, he had felt the same ominous presence as on previous visits.
He had scanned the area and thought he saw something large walking through the trees in the distance.

There had been long tears through his father's shirt and scratches along his back, which seemed to point to a bear, but that idea didn't work with the fallen tree limb. There were also several large round impressions that appeared to resemble large dog tracks near the body, but investigators had suggested that a bear had come by sometime right after Tate had fallen to the ground and tried to attack him, seeing easy prey.

Since then, Jake had done research on Bigfoot and monster sightings in Olympic National Park. While skeptical about the creature, he was open to learning about other people's experiences. He had heard occasional stories from his neighbors, most of whom lived here year-round and spent summer nights sitting by campfires in the back of their property and talking while watching the moonlight and hearing nocturnal animals around them. He was convinced that his father had been killed by Bigfoot, although he had never shared that idea with anyone. The true events of that night would most likely never be known.

He turned off the lights and left the building, making sure the door was firmly locked behind him. He got into his personal truck and turned left out of the station. When he came around a curve in the road, he slowed down to make sure people had left the Marmot Trail. There was no overnight hiking or camping allowed on this three-mile scenic path. No cars remained in the lot, so he drove another half mile before pulling over in front of a gate on the opposite side of the road from the lake.

The signage proclaimed this area to be the Bobcat Lake Research Project. It was four hundred acres of natural forest land that had been set aside for studies. It was true that botanists, geologists, and biologists had once worked here. They often came in to study the areas of the forest that held native plants, many smaller mammals, and interesting rock and land formations. On the other end of the property, a rocky cliff led down to a beautiful valley.

A few months before the fire, the scientists had started

requesting the presence of one of the law enforcement rangers when they were on the land. The project manager, Faye Carson, was one of his neighbors, and she had approached his boss with the request. Jake had not been the only ranger assigned to the role, but he had been there the most frequently since his station was so close to the research area.

He had asked Faye directly one day why she felt that there should be an armed ranger on site. "We're studying plants and animals, and we're not all hunters or comfortable being armed," she had pointed out to him. "We do have some anti-bear items, but there may be something else in there."

"Something else?" Jake had raised his eyebrows. He wondered if Faye was referring to cougars, but the scientists had all been trained on how to handle wildlife sightings. He even wondered if she was referring to Bigfoot.

"Something else," she had repeated, and then had gone off with one of the geologists to look at a new rock formation they had located at the other side of the compound.

All of the scientists had seemed grateful for the presence of the park rangers. Six months after his father had died, the project had been closed down. He had been there the day that the Faye and three researchers had faced an unusual animal encounter. He had been told it was a bear, but the stories that had arisen since then had made him doubt Faye's story.

He had asked Faye again about the encounter, and the project closure. She had told him that there were just one too many unexpected sightings in the project area, and that the smaller animals they had been observing were disappearing. "What encounters? he had pressed. She would only shake her head and ask if he had ever seen an ape-like beast walking through the trees in his direction, larger than any known animal in the forest.

"No," he answered, but the question made him once again think of what he had heard and felt around his dad's cabin. Faye claimed that Bigfoot existed. Although he had never seen the creature, Jake could sometimes bring himself to believe that something monstrous lived in these woods. It was large enough to get over the six-foot chain-link fence that surrounded the four hundred acres of now-empty park service land, and strong enough to have made a couple of dents at the side of the front gate.

No vehicles were in sight near the property, which satisfied Jake. He had set up two trail cameras on one of the trees next to the large metal gate that blocked off access to the land. The fence protected the area, but he knew it was not impossible for a human to find a way inside. He already knew that Cole and Laine were back in town, because the camera had picked them up when they parked along the road yesterday. They had paused at the gate before going away, but had returned for several minutes last night. They had been just at the edge of the camera's view, and now he could see what they had been doing. He stared out of his window at the old sign.

"Bigfoot Ridge," he read, seeing the newly painted letters on the sign. "That ass. This is going to attract some attention for sure."

He got out of the truck and approached the gate. Bigfoot Ridge was a name he had heard before, although it was more connected with another park elsewhere in the country. Cole apparently thought he could draw people here to find whatever creature was lurking inside. Jake shook his head. He'd have to be more vigilant while Cole was around, that was for sure. He checked that the cameras were still working, and then got back into his truck. The second trail camera faced away from the road, where he could monitor it at home or at work, and keep an eye on anything that might come up to the gate from inside the research area.

He pulled out and drove several more miles to his cabin on the lake. He parked in his driveway and waved to Faye Carson, who was standing at her kitchen window, washing dishes. She waved back, and he entered his cabin. He was going to spend the rest of the evening watching television and relaxing in his chair. There was no sign of any strange activity on the camera, so he turned off his monitor. He needed to get away from the job tonight, and hoped that Cole Patterson wouldn't be causing any more trouble during this visit.

CHAPTER 3

"How much longer do you plan to keep doing this, Autumn?" Marcia Hunter asked as she sat down on the couch across from her daughter. "Haven't you put yourself in enough danger?"

"And haven't you finally realized that you're not going to catch a Bigfoot?" her brother, Tom, asked.

Autumn sighed. She had finished packing this morning and included all of her usual Bigfoot hunting gear. This time she had also brought along a notebook to write down her observations and thoughts while she was on her trip. It might be an interesting idea to add a typical cryptid investigation to the book, and she could get pictures from Nate and Mike to add to her own collection when they were done.

Before leaving the house, she had decided to drop by her parents' house and have a brief visit with them. Her brother, Tom, three years younger than Autumn, was currently separated from his wife and sleeping in his old bedroom. He had always been derisive about her interest in Bigfoot, and despite her past interactions with the creature, and dogmen, he refused to believe that she had actually ever seen any monsters. Her parents were more supportive, especially when she had faced difficulties sleeping and kept having visions of a Bigfoot looking in her windows after her first visit to Tahoma Valley.

Her father, Bruce, entered the living room and she stood and gave him a hug. "Hi, Autumn. No Zach today?"

"He's on the road filming for *Creature Hunt*," she reminded him. "I've been placed on furlough from the library for two weeks. When I talked to him last night, he suggested that I use the time to work on our book. I'm on my way up to Bobcat Lake to join Nate, Mike, and Tiffany."

"Oh, great," Tom said. "More crazies. Just what the parks need out there."

"Hush, Tom," Marcia told him. "You didn't answer my question, Autumn."

"How much longer do I plan to do this?" Autumn repeated. "Until I either find scientific proof of Bigfoot that can't be disproven or otherwise explained, or until I just get too old to go out into the forest anymore."

Bruce smiled. "I still think it's kind of funny that you're dating someone whose job is literally chasing after monsters, even if they've never caught one on camera."

Autumn nodded and laughed. "Well, that's how we met."

"How long will you be gone?" Marcia asked.

"Just a few days," Autumn replied. "Nate and Mike have to be back at work on Wednesday." She placed a piece of paper on the living room table. "That area of the peninsula doesn't have great cell reception, so here's the phone number and address of Bobcat Lodge. You can leave a message for me at the front desk if you can't reach me by phone."

"Wasn't that area closed off for a couple of years?" Bruce asked. "Something about needing to repair the trails, I think. There was a fire in the area."

"Yes," Autumn confirmed. "I looked that up last night. There was actually a fire on the lodge grounds, and the former owners sold it last year. The resort re-opened this spring, and Nate and Mike texted last night that the owners claimed it had been a pretty good summer for them."

"I wonder why the former owners took so long to sell it," Bruce said thoughtfully. "There's an area up near Bobcat Lake that used to be used for environmental research. You know, native plants, rocks, local animals, that kind of thing. People at work were surprised by its closure." Bruce Hunter worked in the facilities department at a private college that had several strong environmental science programs.

"Maybe the fire was caused by Bigfoot," Tom laughed. "Trying to keep people like you out." He shook his head. "It's more likely monster hunters like you and your friends couldn't control a campfire."

"Tom, maybe you should go check on breakfast," Marcia said. Tom looked like he wanted to argue, but left the room. Marcia gave Autumn a sympathetic look.

"Be careful out there, dear," she said to her daughter. "You know I worry whenever you go out looking for Bigfoot or anything else that's out there."

"I'll stay with my friends," Autumn assured her. She meant it. She didn't want to go out into Olympic National Park by herself. She had heard too many stories about animal encounters there to think that a solo hike would be a good idea.

"Good to hear," Bruce said.

"Breakfast is ready," Tom called from the kitchen.

"Have some food before you go," Marcia urged. Autumn smelled her favorite breakfast casserole and nodded. She joined her family at the dining room table, and the rest of their conversation stayed far away from monsters and the paranormal.

An hour later, with a bag of snacks provided by her parents despite her brother's snide comments about her possibly regaining the thirty pounds she had lost last year, Autumn drove out of Tacoma and turned on some of her favorite music. She spent the next couple of hours driving along Highway 101. It had been several years since she had last visited the Olympic Peninsula, and she wanted to enjoy the trip.

She noticed a sign for a scenic overlook and decided to get some pictures. She pulled in and parked at the edge of a small parking lot. There was only one other car there, but it was empty. She got out of her vehicle, leaving the passenger side window down for some fresh air, and stretched. Several signs were posted along the chain link fence that separated a lawn from the edge of the cliff. She read them, noting the standard warnings about not climbing over the fence and being careful while walking on the trail to the overlook.

She brought her camera with her as she set out down the trail. It was a pleasant ten-minute walk along a clear dirt path. Autumn stopped a couple of times along the way to take pictures of what appeared to be an empty forest. A couple of times on her walk, bushes along the path rustled, but when a squirrel appeared and ran away, she laughed and shook her head. It was a hazard of her hobby that she was always looking for signs of big animals. Sometimes the littlest creatures also caused big distractions.

She reached the overlook and stood still, staring in awe at the scene before her. Mountains rose up sharply from the landscape. Trees closer to her, below the overlook, were enveloped in the shades of brown, yellow, and red that occurred every fall. Some of the mountain peaks were already topped with snow. The rain forest environment closer to the mountain the slopes dark green and looked mysterious and foreboding from this distance. She could see a lake and a stream snaking through the valley immediately beneath her. It was the perfect environment for all sorts of creatures. It was the perfect environment for Bigfoot.

She held up the camera and snapped away. Taking some time to walk along the edge of the fence to get different angles, she stopped at the end of the overlook and glanced down at the ground. Was that a footprint? A large footprint?

Autumn started getting nervous and wondered about the occupants of the other car she had seen. In her time at the overlook, she had not seen or heard any other people. She got a shot of the track and looked as far into the forest as she dared to go from here. Her parents' warning about not going off by herself was fresh in her head, and this was not the place to suddenly start wandering off the trail.

A shout caught her attention. Then, a scream. She turned and hurried back along the trail that had led to the overlook.

When she reached the parking lot, she saw two women standing near the other car, looking off into the forest behind the lot. She ran over to them. "Hi. Is something wrong?"

"Is that your car?" one of the women asked, pointing to Autumn's Honda.

"Yes, it is."

"There's a port-a-potty down that way," the other woman said, pointing to the area near the road. Autumn looked over and saw the outhouse. It was green and nearly hidden from this vantage point. "We were just coming back from using it when we saw…something…standing at your window."

"My window?" Autumn turned and remembered she had left her passenger window down. She hurried to the car and saw that the bag of apples her mother had given her had been torn apart. Apples were all over the footwell, but she could tell that some had been taken.

"It was ugly," the first woman said, her voice breaking. "Tall, and wide. And hairy."

"Maybe it was Bigfoot," the second woman said, appearing to try to tease her partner out of her fright.

"That's a myth."

"What else do you think it was?"

"Thanks for telling me," Autumn interrupted quietly. She returned to the SUV and opened the passenger door. She started to gather the remaining apples and placed them in a box.

With the excitement over, the two women got into their car and sped out of the parking lot. Autumn waited until they were out of sight, then retrieved the apples and dumped them by a bush. "It's for you!" she called out, then rearranged the rest of the snacks in their bags and drove away. She wanted to get to the lake, and it was already early afternoon. Whatever animal had grabbed her apples, she would let them enjoy the rest of the day in peace.

28

CHAPTER 4

"John! Wait for me!"

John Britten turned around to see his sister, Beth, stepping through the same bushes where he had just walked. "I thought we were going to stay on the Marmot Trail," Beth complained when she reached him. "There are supposed to be great views from the top of the ridge up there."

"I want to see if those footprints are still here," John said. He had set out to hike the trail on his own yesterday, but he had been curious about the chain-link fence that he could see through the woods near the parking lot. Despite warnings to stay on the path, he had hiked to the fence and tried to see what there could be on the other side that was worth the barrier. Not noticing anything but trees and plants, he had turned around and looked down.

There had been large footprints on his side of the fence. John went hiking a lot, and he had never seen any tracks like these before, but he had heard stories about people finding them. It was a similar shape to a human foot, but when he put his own foot inside the track, he whistled. He was six feet, four inches tall, and these prints were probably five times the size of his own foot, even including his hiking boots. He had taken a couple of pictures with his camera and gone back to the trail. Instead of continuing on his hike, he had gone back to the hotel in Port Mason where he was staying with his family.

Beth was not an adventurous person. She liked going for walks in a park near her house where there was a flat paved trail circling the sports fields and playground. She definitely didn't believe in anything like ghosts or monsters, and adamantly refused to believe in the Northwest legends of Bigfoot. John was more open to the idea of the creature existing, but he usually kept his thoughts about it to himself. When he had told Beth about the footprints, and showed her the pictures, she had rolled her eyes. "Yeah, right. That's probably just someone using a fake device they made to fool people."

"Off the trail? Why not put them where people would notice?"

She shrugged. "I don't know. I don't believe they're real footprints."

"I didn't finish my hike. Want to go with me tomorrow?"

Beth was twenty, and John was twenty-three. Their parents had decided to take them on some family vacations before both kids were done with college and starting careers and new lives. This trip to the Olympic Peninsula was one of several trips that had been planned in the past couple of years. Unfortunately, their father had broken his ankle last week and their mother wanted to stay home and take care of him. They had urged John and Beth to go on the trip, anyway, as the hotel and some activities had already been planned and paid for.

To his surprise, Beth had asked him about the Marmot Trail. He gave her the guidebook that explained that the trail was only three miles long, an easy path with a gradual elevation that ended in a point overlooking the Olympic Mountains. She had agreed, as she often walked three or miles in the park.

Now, he hoped he could find the footprints and prove to her that they existed. "They were next to the fence over here," he said, seeing the area where he had been yesterday.

To his dismay, there was no sign of the footprints. Something had walked over the area where they had been and other tracks, more recognizable as local animals, were in the dirt. "I swear, they were here."

"Uh huh." Beth didn't sound like she believed him, but he was grateful that she didn't tell him he had been a fool for thinking they might be Bigfoot tracks.

A scream startled them. Beth dropped her water bottle and swore. John spun in a circle, trying to figure out where the sound had originated. It hadn't sounded like a woman screaming, but he didn't think it was an animal.

The scream came again, this time from somewhere on the other side of the fence. A roar sounded in response. "Holy hell," Beth said. "What's going on in there?"

John started walking along the edge of the fence. "Come on, let's find out."

Beth stared at him, but then followed her brother. He had spent a lot more time hiking and camping than she had, and she trusted that he wouldn't lead them into danger. They walked for what seemed like half a mile, listening as the screams moved along with them. Beth thought she could feel some shaking on the ground, but it didn't feel like an earthquake. The whole situation was surreal to her.

They stopped walking when they suddenly reached a cliff. It was a rocky outcropping, with about a fifty-foot drop to the valley below. It was there that they saw the animal that had made the screaming noises. It was a cougar, limping badly, and bleeding, making its way down the rocks.

John pulled himself up onto the nearest boulder. "What are you doing?" Beth hissed. "Get down."

He shook his head. "Better view. The cougar just reached the ground."

He reached his hand to Beth. She hesitated, then took it and let him help her up onto the rock. They stood silently and watched as the large cat staggered across the shallow grass. It turned around and looked back up at the cliff and made a sound that resembled the screaming they had heard, with a growling undertone. That was a more familiar call to John.

Whatever had attacked the cougar had apparently retreated, because the cat's cries were met with silence. It continued walking in the direction of another forested area on the far side of the clearing. John felt bad for the animal, and hoped its injuries weren't life-threatening.

"What is that?" Beth asked slowly. She pointed to a dark shape that was sitting quietly near a tree that the cougar was passing. From here, it appeared to be a large coyote, maybe even a wolf. "Is that some sort of dog?"

"I'm not sure," John said. They watched as the cougar finally reached the trees and, with one last look across the field, disappeared from sight.

It was then that John and Beth got the biggest shock of their lives. The wolf-like creature slowly rose from its hiding place, standing on its hind legs and stretching slowly upwards until it reached a height of roughly seven feet. John knew his guess might be wrong, but he tried to use the trees next to the creature as a guide. He had never heard of a wolf acting like this, and his first instinct was to grab Beth's hand and run.

"Wait," she said. She seemed entranced by the creature. "Look at its legs. Don't they seem backward to you? How can it walk?"

The creature answered them by taking several steps forward. It flexed large paws that, from their vantage point, seemed to end in long fingers, almost like a human. "It's going after the cougar, isn't it?" Beth suddenly asked, her panicked voice loud in the silence.

The creature seemed focused on stalking the cat. It walked, its long snout sniffing the air, to the tree where they had last seen the cougar. Then, the creature vanished, suddenly breaking into a sprint while still on its hind legs. They heard a distant scream, and then silence.

"Oh my God. What was that?"

"I don't know," John answered honestly. "Come on. Let's get out of here. I think we should be around other people right now."

"And what animal here would take on a cougar, anyway?

I mean, I get that there may be bears, but attacking a cougar? It would have to be a carnivore, right?" Beth rambled on as she followed him through the forest. She fell silent, and they finally emerged back onto the Marmot Trail.

"Do you want to finish the hike?" he asked with a weak laugh.

"Not today," Beth said. "I want to get back to the hotel and stay by the pool for the rest of the afternoon."

John agreed. There weren't many things that could scare him about the forest. Seeing something like an upright walking wolf, and a cougar that had been attacked by another animal with a loud roar and the ability to shake the ground, had certainly challenged his senses for the day. They managed to smile and nod at people passing by them in the opposite direction. Part of John wanted to warn the hikers about what might be out there, but he had no idea what he could say that wouldn't sound crazy.

They placed their backpacks in the trunk and John started his car. Down the road, he stopped at the ranger station. "We should tell them we saw a limping and bleeding cougar in that valley," he said. "Nothing else."

Beth nodded. "Nothing else. That stays between us."

I'm also saying something about it on that online forum I joined last month, John thought to himself. Beth had no idea that he had sought out stories on the internet about Bigfoot and other monsters. He had posted the tracks online yesterday.

They walked into the ranger station. Beth seemed to visibly calm down at the sight of two uniformed rangers. "Hello," John said. "I'm John. This is my sister, Beth. We were just down at the Marmot Trail, and looked down into the valley below it. We happened to see a cougar down there. It was limping, and I think it had been recently injured because I thought I saw blood."

"On the Marmot Trail," echoed one of the rangers. His

name badge read J. Tyler, and he wore a belt that included a gun and other law enforcement equipment.

John nodded. "Yes. We thought we'd stop in and report it."

"Thank you," said the other ranger, a young Black man, who was sitting at the information desk. "We'll look into it."

"Thanks," John said. "Oh, we heard the cougar screaming before we saw it. Maybe it was trying to fight back against whatever was attacking it."

"Attacking it?" Jake asked.

"And then there was the wolf," Beth said nervously. "It followed the cougar."

Aaron shook his head. "There are no wolves in Olympic National Park."

"We saw one," she insisted. "It was walking on its hind legs."

Both rangers stared at her. She looked away, rubbing her hands together. John put his hand on her shoulder and nodded at the two men. "Have a nice day," John said, and opened the front door. Beth smiled nervously at the rangers and followed her brother outside.

Jake smiled grimly and looked out the front window of the station. The siblings seemed to be arguing about something as they returned to their car. "Something made those two nervous."

"I've been up and down the Marmot Trail many times," Aaron said. "And there's no place along the path where you can get a clear view down in the valley that would lead to seeing a cougar closely enough to see blood on its body."

"They were off-trail," Jake agreed. "Probably followed the Bobcat Lake Project fence to the cliff."

"Should we send someone out to check on their story?"

Jake shook his head. "If its injuries are bad enough, it'll die out in the forest. Nature will take care of it."

A family stepped inside the station. Aaron greeted them

while Jake retreated to his office. He wondered what had attracted John and Beth to the project area. Shaking his head, he looked down at the paperwork that needed to be filled out today. He sat down and checked the trail cameras, but didn't see anything that could explain the cougar. He also wondered what they might have seen that would give them the idea of a wolf. A coyote, maybe. He shook his head, picked up his pen, and started on the work that needed to be done today.

CHAPTER 5

Autumn made one more stop on the road to Bobcat Lake, at a small gift shop that seemed to cater to the Bigfoot-loving crowd. The inside of the shop was set up exactly as she had suspected it would be. A seven-foot-tall statue of the monster. Shelves of various small items that featured the monster. And a section of books on the creature and other cryptids, even including a field guide journal that Bigfoot hunters could use if they were going out looking for the creature.

Autumn imagined her book here someday. She would remember to keep notes during her time in the Olympic Mountains so that she could include the field investigation section. Zach had promised that he would do the same during one of the *Creature Hunt* episodes this season, although he didn't tell her which creature he would be documenting. She liked that element of surprise, since their book was about more creatures than Bigfoot.

There were several books by someone named Cole Patterson. She had heard the name before, so she picked up one of them and opened it. Inside were several stories about cryptid sightings all over the country, including some nameless horrifying creatures she had never heard of until now. She put the book down and looked around some more. There were several postcards that featured the park and various locations, so she decided to purchase a couple of them with pictures of Bobcat Lake.

She left the store with the postcards and a sweatshirt, putting it on before returning to her car. The temperature had fallen during her drive. She spent the last thirty minutes on the road trying to pay attention to traffic while also admiring the short glimpses she was getting of the lake.

When she found the turnoff for the cabins, excitement welled up inside her. She parked and walked to the lodge. It was an enormous three-story building, made to look like a log cabin. There was a central portion with a large doorway and windows from floor to ceiling on each side. Two wings on either side of the building contained rooms for people who didn't want to stay in one of the cabins that were set along the shoreline.

Autumn followed a path along the side of the building that gave her a view of the lake. It was a beautiful, clear, body of water, and she knew it was the second-deepest lake in the state. She saw several boats out on the water, and the resort had a dock across from the lodge with some rowboats and canoes that looked to be available to rent. She looked to her right and left, and could see several cabins in both directions.

She was about to try to call her friends when she heard a familiar voice shout her name. She turned to see Mike waving at her from the front of the lodge. "Hi!" she said, hugging him when she reached him. "I was going to call you."

"The reception's not very good out here," he reminded her. "The lodge has wi-fi, though, and a couple of computer and library rooms we can use. The cabins have very basic channels."

"I bet that's driving Nate crazy."

"Not as much as you'd might think. Remember, we've spent a lot of time in the RV with no television at all."

"True," Autumn conceded. "Do I need to check in?"

"Yeah. We told the owners you were coming. We need to get a key for you, and they have this welcome packet for all the guests." He guided her through the lodge door. "Just wait until we have dinner in the restaurant here. You won't be disappointed."

She paused when she walked through the door. A high ceiling was lined with wooden beams that met in the center of the room. Lights lined the beams, giving the large lobby a soft glow. One side of the lobby led to a hallway with public rest rooms, a gift shop, and a small coffee bar. The other side of the lobby had a doorway that led to the restaurant, with the doors currently closed. A fireplace was located near the entrance with a stone chimney going through the ceiling. Another hallway led past the dining room, and signs for computer rooms and a library were posted on the wall.

She studied the large staircase that led up to the second floor. The wood banisters were polished, and the posts at the bottom of the stairs featured Native American carvings. She heard people talking and turned to face the check-in desk, which was tucked into a recessed portion of the wall. Mike guided her over to the desk, where a man and a woman stood, looking over several pieces of paper.

"Hi, Jenna," Mike said. "Our fourth guest is here. This is Autumn Hunter."

"Hi, Autumn," the woman greeted her. She looked to be in her late forties, with wavy brown hair and green eyes. She was short, almost a foot shorter than the similarly-aged man next to her. They were both wearing jeans and polo shirts with the Bobcat Lodge logo. "I'm Jenna Stalberg. I manage the lodging side of this resort. This is my husband, Donnie. He manages the restaurant and gift shop."

"Nice to meet you," Donnie said. "Are you a Bigfoot hunter, too?"

"We already told them why we were here," Mike explained to Autumn.

"Yes," she replied to Jenna and Donnie. "I hear this area could have a few of them."

"You're hardly the first people to be here for that reason," Jenna said. She turned to the mailbox behind her labeled "Cabin Ten" and retrieved an envelope. "There's even a camp about an hour away that claims they can guarantee people have a Sasquatch sighting."

"Bold claim," Autumn noted. She thanked Jenna for the envelope and opened it to take a brief look at the contents. There was a brightly colored map of the resort, a sheet listing the rules of the property, and a book of coupons for towns along Highway 101. "It's not that easy to just go out and find one."

Mike bit back a smile. Autumn knew he was thinking about some of their recent adventures. "Well, Nate and I have already encountered two people here that claim to have knowledge of a place where the creatures have been seen more frequently in the last year. They refused to say anything else about it. They also said that the area was being referred to by other people with a different name, but didn't say what it was."

"The Bobcat Lake Project Bigfoot story is going around again?" Donnie asked. He moved away from the desk. "Cole Patterson and Laine Dawson, I presume?"

"Yes," Mike replied. "We were chatting with them at breakfast about various hiking trails."

"Be careful around those two," Jenna advised. "They've already been here a few times this year, getting people worked up about seeing something called a Batsquatch."

Donnie laughed loudly. "A Bigfoot with wings. Not likely."

Autumn met Mike's eyes and knew they'd be discussing it later. "Well, I'd like to get settled into the cabin," she said. "What time does the restaurant open?"

"At five, in about an hour," Donnie said. "I better get in there. Got some things to do."

"If you need anything, the evening receptionist comes on at seven," Jenna said. "I'm usually back in my office or wandering around the grounds when I'm not at the desk, but there's always someone here if you need something."

"Thanks."

Autumn and Mike left the lodge and Autumn shivered in the afternoon breeze. "Let's get your bags to the cabin. We have to walk them over."

"No problem."

Autumn retrieved her bags and locked her SUV, then followed Mike past the lodge and down a paved pathway. A few people were just coming in off the lake, adding to the pile of canoes on the dock. Lifejackets hung in a covered shelter, along with oars and safety gear. Other people were sitting at tables scattered on the grassy shores of the lake. A beach area was not currently occupied, but chairs and a firepit indicated that it was a frequent meeting place.

"We have a firepit outside the cabin," Mike told her, following her gaze. "We sat out there last night and talked to other guests when they walked by. This is a pretty active place. I'm surprised at the amount of people around this time of year, to be perfectly honest."

"I agree. I figured it would be nearly deserted."

They reached the cabin, which was marked with numerals on a post lining the porch. Mike opened the door, and Autumn stepped inside, grateful for the warm air that surrounded her. Tiffany and Nate pulled their eyes from the television show they were watching.

"Autumn! I'm so glad you were able to come," Tiffany said as she stood and hugged Autumn. "Although I hate the reason."

"Two-week furlough?" Nate agreed as he also hugged her. "Well, their loss. Let me show you to your room."

He strode over to a narrow staircase, thankfully with a railing, that led to the loft. She followed him up, gently dragging her bag behind her. When they reached the top, she sank onto the bed.

The cabin reminded her of the ones she had stayed in at Mitzi's Cabin Resort in Tahoma Valley. The bed in the loft was made of wood, and included a twin mattress that was comfortable for her, and several pillows. Sheets and a nice quilt were on the bed. A dresser sat against the wall. Nate opened a door nearby. "You have a half bath up here. There's a full bath downstairs between the bedrooms with a shower. Just let us know when you want to use it."

Autumn nodded and stood. She tugged at a heavy curtain and pulled it across the loft. It shielded the bed and bathroom from view of anyone downstairs, but stopped short of the staircase. She looked out the window and was pleased to discover that she had a view of the forest. "Is that a walking path there?" she asked, pointing to a dirt trail that was marked with a couple of signs. "That guests can use?"

"Yep. I think that one is called the Geoduck Trail. We were planning to go take a look at that one and another trail tomorrow."

"Cool."

"We already put some cameras up outside," Mike called from the bottom of the stairs. "And there's one in your window."

"Motion sensor operated?" she asked, seeing the camera mounted to the upper window ledge.

"Yes," Nate confirmed.

"Okay. Let me do some unpacking and I'll join you all downstairs."

"Don't take too long," Mike called up the stairs. "I'm getting hungry."

She laughed. Nate left the loft and she kept the privacy curtain in place while she changed into a new pair of jeans and a long-sleeved shirt. She placed clothing in the dresser doors and used the bathroom, washing her face and brushing her hair. She already felt better after her long drive.

She went back downstairs with the bags of snacks from her parents and told her friends about her encounter at the overlook. "It just took some apples. Not anything that was in the plastic bags." She unpacked the snacks. Granola bars, M&Ms, a bag of clementines, and some crackers and cheese. "Maybe that bag was just easier to get into?"

"Or easier to smell," Tiffany pointed out. She opened the

bag of M&Ms and poured some out into her hand. "So, you left the rest of the apples?"

"Yes."

"Did you see any footprints?" Nate asked.

"I didn't even think to look," she admitted. "As soon as the other two women left, I just wanted to get out of there myself."

They chatted for another thirty minutes, and then Mike pointed to the clock. "It's dinner time."

"Okay, okay," Nate laughed. "Grab your coats, everyone. Let's go enjoy an evening in the lodge."

CHAPTER 6

"This is nice," Autumn said an hour later, when she and her friends were finishing their meal. They had arrived at the lodge and waited for about fifteen minutes before being seated in the dining room. Mike had been right about there being a surprising amount of people here for early October, but she reasoned that it was a Saturday. Most people were likely out here for the weekend and the resort would probably be quieter by Monday.

Tiffany nodded. "When we checked in yesterday, Jenna said that they had just reopened the lodge in April after purchasing the resort from the previous owners."

"I wonder what happened to make it close down?" Nate asked.

"I can answer that for you," Donnie said. He seemed to appear out of nowhere. "How was your dinner?"

"Delicious," Autumn said. She had decided on a simple meal, and ordered the pasta alfredo. It had been one of the best dishes she had ever tasted.

Everyone else agreed. "Jenna and I actually bought this place last October," Donnie told them. "It was shut down for a little over two years. At first, it was closed because of a fire along one of the trails that destroyed a couple of cabins and some other buildings on the property. The owners could have opened the lodge and some of the cabins, but then something else came along that frightened them away."

"Frightened them away?" Tiffany asked nervously.

"They never told us what it was. They just said that there was something on the grounds that didn't belong here and they were no longer interested in keeping the business alive. Jenna and I had both worked at hotels back when we were in college, so we decided it was a good time to leave our other careers and branch out on our own. We left the destroyed buildings in place and repaired the cabins. We redecorated everything, added the coffee bar and gift shop, and opened in time for people to start making plans for their summer vacation to the park."

"You said it's been successful," Mike said.

"Yes. We've had some occasional stories of people feeling that they were being watched out in the forest. And like Jenna mentioned when Autumn checked in, a few people have said that they heard and saw a flying monster in the forest behind the cabins."

Autumn noticed a couple at a nearby table also listening to Donnie's story. They glanced at her, then at each other. Donnie looked over at them. "Hi, Cole. Hi, Laine. Nice to see you back."

"Thanks, Donnie," the man said. He stood up, taking one last sip of his soda. Autumn guessed that he was Cole Patterson. She wondered if he was the author of the books that she had seen at the gift shop. "Let's get going, Laine."

The woman nodded and got up from the table, collecting her jacket. The couple left and Donnie turned back to Autumn's table. "Flying monster?" Nate prompted.

"Oh, yes. Just some nonsense, I think, but people have really seemed like they believe what they're saying. Oddly enough, the stories are always more frequent after those two are here for a few days." He gestured at the backs of Laine and Cole.

"Do you think there are Bigfoot out here?" Autumn asked directly.

Donnie smiled. "It's kind of hard to answer that question. We've certainly hosted enough people this year that have come to look for Bigfoot. And of course, we take advantage of the Bigfoot legend in our gift shop like most tourist-oriented places in Washington."

He gestured to the departing couple. "You should talk to Cole and Laine. They have some stories to tell."

"Thanks for the suggestion," Mike replied.

Donnie looked around. "I better check on some other guests. Let one of my staff members know if you need anything." He nodded at the table and moved to another area of the restaurant.

"What's the plan for the rest of the night?" Tiffany asked. "Is there anything going on here?"

"Let's check the calendar in the lobby," Nate replied, taking her hand and getting up from the table.

Autumn and Mike followed. Autumn stepped aside when they got to the lobby and tried to call Zach. She reached his voice mail and let him know she had arrived at the resort. "And I've already seen some possible Bigfoot action," she laughed. "Call me when you can."

She joined her friends in front of a large bulletin board near the entrance. "There's a sing-along down at the beach," Mike suggested.

"Pass," Tiffany said.

"Card and board games are available in the library," Autumn pointed out. "Have any of you been there yet?"

"No. Let's go check it out," Tiffany said.

Mike led the group down the hall to a large room. Two walls were lined with bookshelves. Four tables were set up in the middle of the room with lamps in the center of each table, although there were also overhead lights. Another wall featured shelves filled with decks of cards and game boxes that could be checked out for a couple of days through a sign-up sheet on the wall. "I thought there were some computers here," Nate said.

Tiffany gestured to an open doorway in the other wall. "In there."

They looked through the doorway and found four computer desks with desktop computers. A map of the Olympic National Park covered the upper half of another wall. Two people were already in the room. They turned and looked at the newcomers.

"Hi," Cole said. He stepped closer to Autumn. "I met your friends earlier today. I'm Cole Patterson. This is my girlfriend, Laine Dawson."

To Autumn, they appeared to be the typical fit hiking enthusiasts that she pictured out in the park during the warm days of summer. "Hi," she replied. "I'm Autumn Hunter. Your name sounds familiar. Have you ever written a book?"

"Several of them," he replied with a smile. "So, you know that I'm interested in cryptids. All types, not just the standard Bigfoot stories."

"We overheard your conversation with Donnie at dinner," Laine said. "And we think we know what scared away the former owners."

"What's that?" Mike said.

"Let's go in the other room and sit down," Cole suggested. When they were settled at a table in the library, he studied each of them. "We didn't discuss this at breakfast this morning, but are you really here looking for Bigfoot?"

"What gave that away?" Nate asked.

Cole shrugged. "We've stayed at various locations around the peninsula long enough that we now separate most people into three categories. Romantic weekends away in a forest cabin, hikers looking for their next greatest challenge, and people looking for monsters."

"And we're monster people," Tiffany said.

Laine nodded. "We can give you some information on places you might want to look. Cole and I have been coming out to Bobcat Lake and the surrounding areas for almost two years." She pulled a business card out of her pocket and handed it to Autumn.

Autumn was surprised to see that Laine was the assistant manager of a well-known casino hotel located a couple of hours away, on the coast. Cole also handed her a card. She was not surprised to notice that, along with being an author, he listed his job as a social media influencer.

"What do you think scared off the previous owners?" Autumn asked, handing the cards over to Mike. As he read them, she reached into her fleece jacket and pulled out a small notebook and pen, ready to take notes.

"It's not a monster that most people talk about, but it's possible there's a Batsquatch in the forest," Cole said, his body language and tone serious.

"Batsquatch," Nate repeated. "I've only heard about that cryptid a couple of times, mostly connected with Mount Rainier and Mount Saint Helens."

Autumn kept her mouth shut as she wrote "Batsquatch" in her notes. Zach had been nearly certain that he had seen one near Mount Saint Helens earlier in the year. If there was one here, it would be nice to try to get a photo of it, or some other evidence.

"The hotel where I work hosts an annual Bigfoot conference," Laine said. "In the seven years I've been there I've met a lot of people who describe something similar to what could be called a Batsquatch. I've heard talk about a dogman, but I'm not sure I believe that there would be one in Washington."

Autumn bit her lip and saw Nate and Mike give each other a glance. They had been involved in a personal encounter with a dogman just a little over a month ago in Tahoma Valley, near Mount Rainier. "It's good to keep an open mind," Nate said. Tiffany pulled out a chair and sat down.

"You should take a walk on some of the trails around the resort," Laine said. "They're all fully groomed paths that lead back to the main lodge and parking lot, so you won't get lost. One the path closest to our cabin, you can see one of the buildings that was burned in the fire. There's a spookiness to that building that isn't anywhere else on these grounds. You may find something hiding there."

"Have you actually seen anything that would indicate a Batsquatch?" Mike asked.

"Some glowing red eyes high up in the trees. Rustles of what could be wings when the eyes disappear. Shaking branches, but no sign of any animals coming down a tree trunk," Cole said. "Put it together, and it's a possibility."

"Why do you assume there's no dogman here?" Autumn asked. "This would be a good spot for it. People already laugh off Bigfoot stories, but I know that there aren't any wolves around here. People seeing an upright walking wolf-looking creature might be taken a little more seriously."

"No one takes stories like that seriously around here, especially the park rangers," Cole said. "I tried to interview some people in a neighborhood across the lake, people whose families have been here for years, and one of the rangers asked me to leave. There's a sense over there that something is wrong, and I think maybe it's because they live so close to the few hundred acres of park service research area that were closed down a couple of years ago."

"Research area?" Mike asked. Autumn's ears perked up. Her dad had mentioned that such a place had closed down around here. Maybe she and her friends could figure out why that had happened.

"Have you ever heard of Bigfoot Ridge?" Cole asked.

"No," they replied in unison. Autumn was certain that it was a name that that she had not heard before in connection with Washington. There were other locations in the United States with that name, but she was surprised to learn that there was one here.

"More and more people have taken to calling that research area 'Bigfoot Ridge.' It's four hundred acres of land on the other side of the lake, between the Marmot Trail and that neighborhood I told you about."

"There have always been stories of Bigfoot sightings around the hot springs, in the opposite direction, as well," Laine added. "I'm sure you've heard about the natural thermal springs about thirty minutes south of here."

"Yes," Tiffany said. "Is that a long hike up to the hot springs, once you get to the trailhead?"

"You can check it out on the map. The road that used to lead up there got washed away in a flood a few years ago. That didn't stop people from hiking in anyway, so the state finally built a footbridge. There's a camping area on the way up, but no one can stay overnight. I don't know why anyone would want to stay there."

"Let's get back to this Bigfoot Ridge. Have there been incidents over there?" Autumn asked.

"I haven't heard that someone has actually had a Bigfoot

encounter there," Cole admitted. "There's a spooky feeling about the place. There have been noises from within the fence that surrounds the ridge, like roars and growls. I once tried a couple of wood knocks on a tree along the road. Something started creeping along the fence, but whatever was making those bushes shake didn't reveal itself. Also, the scientists working there just agreed to abandon their projects one day. There are probably still pieces of samples they were taking or tests that they were doing somewhere inside the property. The park rangers monitor the area, but no one's going to get anything out of those guys."

"The area around the hot springs has more recent reports, probably because there are more people hiking around there," Laine said.

"We're members of the Bigfoot Online Group," Autumn commented. "I don't recall any place in the state being referred to as Bigfoot Ridge."

Cole shrugged. "I can't explain that."

"If people aren't going into Bigfoot Ridge now, that may have emboldened whatever animals are there, natural or otherwise. Or maybe it was the animals that caused them to leave in the first place," Mike pointed out

Laine nodded. "That's been our theory, too."

"You should go check out the ridge," Cole urged. "Like I said, we've already been up there this year, poking around the fence. I think there were a couple of large footprints on the other side. But I guess most people find footprints boring by now."

Autumn disagreed. She never found anything that could indicate the presence of Bigfoot to be boring. She always documented as much as she could. Even if the print could be attributed to a bear after being shown to people, it proved that there were large animals in the area. Some people had been known to see bears in various positions and think they might be Bigfoot.

Laine checked her watch. "We're going to join the sing-along at the beach. See you later."

She and Cole left, leaving Autumn and her friends in the library. "They were very helpful," Tiffany said.

"Almost too helpful," Nate said. "I like it when people share information. It kind of seems, though, like we're being directed to a Bigfoot hot spot for a purpose."

"The hot springs, or Bigfoot Ridge?" Autumn asked. "The ridge seems like the place we should go investigate."

"If we go, we're going during the day," Tiffany flatly replied. "There's no way I'm taking a chance on getting stuck anywhere in the Olympic National Park at night."

"Agreed," Nate said. "How about Monday? I'd like to take a walk around the resort tomorrow, and investigate a little closer to the cabin. Maybe we can determine if there's something to that Batsquatch story."

"Sounds good," Mike said. "In the meantime, we're still facing the question of what to do tonight."

Autumn checked her watch. "I vote we go back to the cabin and maybe just watch TV or play a game. I want to get to bed early tonight."

They picked out a board game and left the lodge. On the way back to their cabin, they passed the beach. The sing-along was just about to get started. She didn't see Cole or Laine in the crowd, and assumed that the couple had changed their mind. When they returned to cabin, they stayed up until ten, laughing and chatting over the game and an old show that had always been one of Mike's favorite comedies to watch.

When Autumn changed into her pajamas and turned off the light in the loft, she looked out the window. The resort seemed to be quiet. She saw the red light on the camera turn on and studied the trees. She thought she saw the appearance of two glowing red eyes, but she wasn't sure. She backed away and pulled the curtain shut, making sure to not cover the camera. She crawled into bed and pulled the quilt over her head, hoping for good dreams.

CHAPTER 7

Autumn woke up the next morning to the smell of coffee and the sound of Nate and Mike trying to keep their voices low downstairs. She got out of bed and studied herself in the bathroom mirror. *I'll take a shower this afternoon when we're done exploring*, she told herself. She got dressed and brushed her teeth and hair, then walked down the staircase, hanging onto the railing as she descended.

She heard the shower running. Mike nodded at her and raised his voice from the whispers he and Nate had been exchanging. "Good morning, Autumn. Looks like the sun disappeared for today, but at least it's not raining yet."

She poured herself a cup of coffee and opened the door. Nate and Mike followed her out to the porch. A low mist hung across the lake, although it was possible that would burn off later in the day. She took a deep breath and smelled a fire burning, then turned and noticed a few wisps of smoke coming from the lodge's chimney. The forest along the edge of the resort, and further down around the curve of the lake, looked as dark as she had seen from the overlook yesterday.

"We thought we'd get breakfast at the lodge, then start at one of the trails over on the opposite side of the lake path," Nate said when they returned inside and shut the door. "There are maps available in the lobby."

"Sounds good." Autumn checked her phone and found a voice mail. It was from Zach. She listened to his apology for not answering and encouragement for her trip to the lake. She smiled and saved the message, then put her phone on the coffee table and sat on the couch next to Mike. "How did you sleep?"

"Pretty well," he said. "Did you see anything last night?"

"I looked out my window for a few minutes. Maybe it was just Cole's story getting to me, but I thought I saw red eyes in the trees. I closed the blinds and went to sleep."

"I nodded off right away," Nate said.

"I guess winning three games of Clue will put your mind

at ease," Mike teased.

"I'm pretty good at it," Nate agreed. Autumn smiled. She and Nate had known each other since middle school, and she had played countless rounds of that game with him. She had always been amazed at how quickly his mind worked to put together the solution. As they had grown and discovered a mutual interest in Bigfoot, that talent had led him to often lead their expeditions. She trusted his ability to take in the surroundings and make good judgments of how far they should go.

Everyone in their group had their skills that contributed to their monster-hunting efforts. Erica and Bill not being here this weekend meant that if they were going to do an investigation at Bigfoot Ridge, they'd each have more of a role to play. Mike was often interested doing most of the research behind the places they were going to see, while Autumn and Nate were usually in the lead on the trail. Bill and Erica were often at the back of the group, checking behind them for any clues that they may have missed. Tiffany had only recently started playing more of an active role in the field, but her preferred place was still staying behind in a car or the trailer, keeping in touch with them through whatever means they could use.

Tiffany appeared in the living room. Her pale blonde hair was freshly styled. She wore an outfit similar to Autumn's clothing, without the hiking boots. "After breakfast I'm just going to hang out back here," she told them. Autumn had been expecting that. Tiffany sometimes joined even their most casual hikes, and sometimes just wanted to hang back and keep to herself. "I'll join you tomorrow, though."

"Okay," Nate agreed. They set out for the lodge, running into several other guests along the way. One family, two parents and three kids, were ahead of them going into the lodge. "I want a stuffie!" a young girl exclaimed, trying to pull her mother over to the gift shop. "That stuffie I showed you yesterday!"

"After breakfast," the mother said absently. She turned to

see Autumn closing the door behind her. "Did you hear anything strange last night?"

"No," Autumn replied. "What did you hear?"

"Something howled," a young boy said, standing next to the father. "Not like a wolf, though. It was weird."

"I told you to leave their radio on," the mother said to the father. She looked apologetically at Autumn. "Sorry. It just unnerved us a little. We're leaving today after such a nice week."

The family stepped into the dining room, leaving Autumn and her friends in the middle of the lobby. "A howl?" Nate said. "Not a wolf, I hope. Or a dogman," he finished quietly.

"There are coyotes around here. If there are Bigfoot in the area, though, that might be why the kid thought it sounded odd," Mike said. "That might sound more like a roar, like a primate."

"Can we get breakfast?" Tiffany asked, her stomach audibly growling. Mike led the way into the restaurant.

Breakfast and lunch were both buffet-style, according to the menu posted on the wall at the entrance to the dining room. Autumn gathered her favorite pastry, a cinnamon roll, along with some bacon and eggs. She set her plate down at a table that Mike had already staked out, and went to get orange juice and tea. Her friends found their own food, and they ate with little conversation, instead choosing to listen to the buzz around them.

"A lot of people are checking out today," Nate said when he returned from the buffet. "Cole and Laine are staying for another few days. Jenna stopped by while I was picking out a donut and mentioned that the resort is only half-full during the upcoming week."

"Good. Less people around to run into on the trails," Mike said.

"And more quiet time for me at the cabin," Tiffany added. "Good. I brought a lot of books."

"More Harlequin romances?" Nate laughed. Autumn smiled. Tiffany was always asking her to let her know when the library system received new copies of romance books.

"What else?" Tiffany laughed.

On their way out of the restaurant, they ran into Cole and Laine in the lobby, warming themselves in front of the large fireplace. "Hey, what are you all up to today?" Cole asked.

"Walking around the resort trails," Mike said. They had gathered in front of the resort map, and Autumn retrieved three brochures including the trail system from a nearby stand. On the other side of the lobby, Jenna and another employee were checking out people out the front desk. The gift shop was also buzzing with guests taking home souvenirs from their stay. Autumn saw the little girl getting a stuffed Bigfoot with a funny shirt, and smiled.

"Cool. Have fun. We're in Cabin One if you need anything," Laine said.

"What would we need?" Tiffany asked. Autumn could tell she was growing suspicious of the couple.

Laine shrugged. "You never know what might be out there." She and Cole left the lobby. Nate led the group outside, where they stood off to the side and let other guests wander between the lodge and the parking lot.

"What was that about?" Tiffany muttered.

"Don't let them bother you," Nate said. "Go back to the cabin. Enjoy your day. I'm sure we'll be back before lunch."

"Okay. See you then." She kissed Nate and headed around the side of the lodge.

Autumn, Nate, and Mike had all brought their backpacks to the lodge, so they were ready to go for a hike. *Although hike might not be the best description*, Autumn thought as she looked at the length of the trails. *More like a nature walk.*

She recognized that it was the goal of the resort to create a relaxing atmosphere for their guests while on the property. If guests wanted a challenging trail or whitewater fun, there were other places on the peninsula to find those experiences for a day trip. Here at Bobcat Lodge, the trails were good for wandering through the woods and the lake offered calm and clear waters for boating and swimming. There would be more of a challenge for them tomorrow when they went to seek out Bigfoot Ridge.

"Let's go down to end of the cabins on this side of the lodge and take that trail," Mike suggested. "It's the opposite end of the resort from our cabin and some new scenery for us."

Autumn and Nate agreed. They walked along the cement pathway. The mist was still over the lake, and hovered around the tops of the trees. They reached the trail and found signs labeling this path as the Gray Wolf Trail and warning hikers to stay on the path. Autumn took the lead and walked on the path. She could already tell it was well-maintained and cleared for the safety of the guests. Jenna and Donnie had certainly put all of their efforts into the success of the resort.

The forest was quiet and cool. Ferns and berry bushes lined the path, along with a variety of other plants that Autumn could rarely identify. She looked up and only saw the mist, which made her shiver. She looked back and saw Mike holding his camera up at something off the trail. He started walking again, looking down at whatever image he had captured.

"Building," Nate called out, and pointed. Autumn saw what appeared to be an old cabin. The roof was mostly burned away, but a surprising amount of the structure remained. She saw a smaller trail branching off that led to the structure. She wondered if someone had lived in this cabin when the fire happened, or if it had been used for storage.

"Should we take a look?" she said, gesturing to the mostly overgrown path that led to the cabin.

They looked around and saw no one else around them. "Sure, but let's make it quick," Mike said, taking another look behind them.

"Something out there?" Nate said as they headed off-trail to the cabin.

"Not sure. Maybe that Batsquatch story just got to me. I just feel like something's watching us," Mike admitted.

Autumn and Nate stopped walking. Autumn looked at the

trees where Mike had been pointing his camera. They were too far away for her to tell if she saw an animal, or a human, or if there was just a really odd tree stump out there that looked to be trying to hide next to another tree. "Out there?" she asked quietly, pointing to the trees.

Mike studied his pictures again. "It's probably just a stump."

"Nothing has moved since we've been watching," Nate said. "Come on, let's check out this cabin."

Up close, the cabin was in better shape than Autumn had thought. Although a large portion of the roof had been burned and collapsed, enough remained to still create a sense of shelter. There was a small porch that led to an open doorway. Nate stepped on the porch and saw that the door appeared to have been torn off the hinges and tossed aside into the living room. The door was cracked, and had come to rest against a bookcase that was leaning to one side.

Autumn retrieved a flashlight from her backpack and moved around Nate. She gingerly took a step into the structure and tested the floor. It seemed solid underneath her, and the fire damage looked to have been contained to the upper level of the structure. "I think it's okay," she said, and all of three of them entered the cabin.

"I don't think we're going to find much here," Nate said. "We already knew there were some burned buildings out here. Correction, one burned building. Maybe whatever else was initially damaged finally fell down."

"That would explain the pile of wood off to the right," Autumn said, looking out through a broken window. She saw the charred remains of what had probably been a tool shed roughly fifty feet away.

"Okay, but what happened to the door?" Mike said, gesturing at the hinges.

"Maybe it got blown off in a blast, or was weakened enough by flames to let a strong enough man remove it."

"And this stain on it?" Mike asked, taking a picture. "To be honest, that looks like dried blood."

"It does," Nate admitted.

"And the claw marks?"

"Claw marks?" Autumn and Nate repeated. Mike gestured to the upper area of the door, where four long scratches had been carved into the wood. Autumn shivered.

"This is creepy," she said. She let her flashlight roam around what appeared to be the main room of the cabin. A couch and bookshelves had been left behind, along with a dusty unplugged television set. The bookshelf that was covered by the door was empty, but the others still had books and other small items on them. There was a table near the boarded-up window that had been turned over, and two chairs looked like they had been torn apart. The chair legs were on the other side of the room.

Curious about the rest of the cabin, she ventured over to where a wall separated the front room from the kitchen. She turned a corner and backed away. The ceiling had been half-obliterated by fire, but there was a small pile of something that smelled incredibly bad in the corner.

"Is that…feces?" Nate asked with a disgusted look on his face.

"I think so," Mike replied.

"Want a sample?" Autumn said. She carried plastic vials and bags in her backpack for situations like this. Nate shook his head.

"I think a raccoon or something probably got in here. If there was an animal that caused this damage, there's not going to be any fresh evidence of it. Let's get going." Nate and Mike backed up and took more photos, and then they all left the cabin.

Standing on the porch, Mike pointed. "Okay, the stump is gone."

Autumn looked and saw that whatever had been next to the tree had indeed gone away while they were in the cabin. She shivered. "We can rule out a stump, then, Mike. Whatever it was is obviously alive."

He nodded.

Autumn felt better when they were back on the trail. They continued walking, and after almost another half a mile that took them down a curve through the woods, they emerged from the trees and saw the lodge. The Gray Wolf Trail ended at the parking lot.

"Let's find another trail," Nate suggested. They walked along the edge of the pavement, circling the parking lot, and discovered the Geoduck Trail.

"This looks like it might be longer than the first trail," Autumn said, pointing to the map on the sign.

They were about to set out on the path when they heard a howl in the distance that ended abruptly, as if something had silenced it. The sound sent a shudder down Autumn's spine. She saw a few people getting into their cars pause, listening to see if the sound would come again. When it didn't, everyone started to go about their business, as if nothing unusual had just happened.

CHAPTER 8

"Well, that sounds promising," Nate chuckled nervously. "Come on, let's keep going."

Autumn followed him, with Mike once again bringing up the rear. He kept glancing off to the left side of the trail, which was the more heavily wooded side. For the first few hundred feet of the walk, Autumn was able to get glimpses of the buildings at the resort off to her right, but they soon disappeared. A quarter of a mile into the forest, she heard Mike stop behind her. Nate heard it, too, and turned around.

Mike had his digital camera pointed at something in the distance. "I think there's something out there following us," he stated quietly. Nate and Autumn looked at the picture he had just taken.

She recognized a distinctive tree in the picture as one they had just passed. There was a humanoid figure standing next to it, but she couldn't tell how tall it was because there were no bushes or branches next to it. Nate looked out at the real tree, and there was nothing standing next to it now. "I saw something similar before we reached that burned cabin, and then we saw what we thought was just a stump," Mike said. "But I don't get the sense that it's an animal. It's too short."

"Why would a person be following us?" Autumn asked.

"Maybe to see if we run into something that they're also looking for?" Nate suggested. He frowned. "Like Cole and Laine, perhaps?"

Mike nodded. "If it's an animal, they have dark fur. If it's a person, they're wearing dark clothing. Either way, maybe they'll eventually reveal themselves."

The next several minutes of their walk were uneventful, with no further sightings of the figure they had seen. About halfway down the path, Autumn became frustrated. She picked up a heavy stick from the nearby underbrush and waved it at her friends. "Something howled out here," she said. "Let's see if we can find out what it is."

"Wait," Nate said, but she waved him off. She used both

arms to swing the stick at a tree. Three times in a row, she hit the wood, satisfied with the resulting knocks that sounded through the forest. She stood still after the knocks, waiting for a response.

She and her friends had learned from discussions with other cryptid hunters that primates would use wood knocks to communicate with each other. It was a staple of their investigations now, although usually they were recording and set up in a central area when they started trying to get Bigfoot's attention. She had never done this on a whim before, or when they were this close to other people being able to hear it.

Two knocks sounded in response, and she dropped the stick in surprise. They waited for a couple of minutes, then Autumn picked up the stick again. She was about to knock on another tree when she saw two people emerge from somewhere down the trail. Cole and Laine were dressed in dark green shirts and black pants, both carrying backpacks. "Hey, was that you?" Laine called out, pointing to the stick in Autumn's hand.

"Yes," Nate admitted. "Was that you knocking on a tree that we heard in response?"

"Yep," Cole said. "We got excited for a minute, then saw your jackets through the trees."

"Why have you been following us?" Mike demanded, waving his camera at them. "I have you in pictures from our entire walk this morning."

"We haven't been following you," Laine replied with a frown. "We've been down on this trail for the last hour."

"Did you hear that howl?" Autumn asked, studying their faces closely. She thought she saw a glimmer of fear pass over Laine's expression.

"Yes. That's when we started heading back to the trail, and heard your knocks."

"Anything interesting out there?" Nate said, gesturing to where the couple had entered the trail. There appeared to be nothing beyond them but forest. In that direction, the woods eventually ended at the highway.

"Not really, but we've already explored the resort trails a few times this year," Laine said, shooting Cole a desperate look. She seemed anxious for him to speak up. "So, we went a little deeper through the property today."

"It's kind of risky to be doing wood knocks this close to the resort, isn't it?" Cole said smoothly. "People might get the wrong idea."

"What would be the right idea?" Autumn wondered out loud. "Most people who were here last week have left, and those who are left probably either know about possible ways to make contact with Bigfoot, or don't care about it. They'd probably just hear the knocks as background noise or someone working around the property."

"Maybe," Laine said. "Hey, is it starting to rain?"

Autumn realized that she could feel drops of rain falling on her. "I guess that's all for today," Mike said. Nate and Autumn nodded in agreement. While bad weather wasn't usually a deterrent for outdoor activities in the Pacific Northwest, they hadn't found anything on this trail that might be interesting enough to do more than finish walking the path.

"Let's get back to the cabin," Nate said. Laine and Cole waved and headed back in the direction of the parking lot. Autumn watched until they were out of sight, then grabbed Mike's jacket before he started walking again.

"They were doing something back here," she said. "I don't know what it was, but those two are up to something."

"I don't think there's anything back there," Nate said. "At least, that's what they told us."

"Are you going to just believe them?"

Nate studied her face. "You really think they're lying about something."

"Yes."

"Make a choice," Mike said. "I'd like to get out of the rain. We can come back later. Laine and Cole aren't leaving yet."

"True," Autumn replied. "Let's go. This trail ends near our cabin."

"I do think they're hiding something," Nate assured her as they walked down the path. "But there's no need to go chasing them down when they'll probably end up revealing it to us, anyway. Cole seems like someone who wants to see people's reactions to his work."

They continued down the path, occasionally feeling the rain that they could see falling outside the cover of the trees. Several feet down from where Laine and Cole had emerged from the woods, Autumn stopped and pointed to a tree on the opposite side of the path from where the couple had claimed to be exploring.

There was a sturdy-looking ladder built into the side of the tree, and a structure built around the large trunk. It was a circular platform, made of wood, with a sign attached to the railing. They couldn't read the sign from the base of the tree. "This looks interesting," Mike said. "Shall we go up?"

"I'll give a try." Nate grabbed one of the lower rungs of the ladder and tested it with his full weight. He climbed to the next one, and then hurried up the rest of the ladder to get to the platform. Autumn heard him jump up and down a couple of times and grimaced. He was about twenty feet off the ground.

"Feels solid," he called down. Autumn climbed up and Mike followed. When they had all reached the platform, Autumn was impressed by the view. From here, there were open spots between the trees that gave glimpses of Bobcat Lake, and she could see the roofs of a couple of the cabins. In fact, she thought she recognized their cabin from the shutters outside her loft window.

"I wonder how often people come up here," Mike wondered. "This sign points out the lake view and gives a short history of the lake."

Autumn pulled the map out of her pocket and studied it while Nate and Mike discussed the platform and what use it could have on this tree. She saw that there was a symbol that indicated this platform was aptly called a viewing tower, and discovered that there was another one closer to the end of the path. She told Nate and Mike what she had discovered. "If there's one closer to the end of the trail, wouldn't that have a better view of the lake?"

"Is there one that we missed on the Gray Wolf Trail?" Mike asked, pulling out his camera again and flipping back through the photos.

"I don't remember," Autumn admitted. She had been too fascinated by finding the cabin and looking inside that structure to pay much attention to the surrounding trees.

"Yes," Nate confirmed, looking over Mike's shoulder. "At least, there used to be. See that tree, close to the cabin? There's a ladder running down the trunk."

"Oh, yeah. Are there any more towers on the map, Autumn?"

She scanned the paper. There were two more trails on the property, one much further down the lake from the others. There were two more viewing towers along that trail. "Yep."

"Looks like the rain is starting to come down harder," Mike said, pointing out to the water. "And a bit of wind is kicking up. Let's go get into some dry clothes and get some lunch."

They climbed down from the viewing tower and headed down the trail, looking around through the forest. Near the end of the trail, they found the other viewing tower and Autumn pointed to an unusual addition. "There's a rope attached to that one that goes through the trees," she said.

"That is odd," Mike said. "We should ask Jenna or Donnie about that."

They returned to the cabin and found Tiffany on the couch, watching television with a book open beside her. They all changed into dry clothes. Autumn laid her wet shirt and pants on the dresser to dry, and checked her phone. There was a text message from Zach, asking if she would try to call him again at some point.

"Hey, let's go find lunch somewhere outside the resort,"

she called out, looking down over the railing. "There are a few towns along this highway."

"A lot to choose from," Tiffany agreed. "We passed a couple of diners on our way back from Port Mason yesterday."

Nate looked at map he picked up from the table. "How about here, in Timber Creek. It's right at the highway turnoff to Port Mason."

They walked to the parking lot and waved to Jenna as they passed the front doors of the lodge. She was standing outside, talking to a park ranger, and waved back at them. The ranger turned to look at them as they passed, and Autumn wondered why he had come to the resort. Jenna seemed relaxed and was laughing at something the ranger said to her, so she shrugged it off and got into Mike's SUV with her friends.

Fifteen minutes later, they pulled into the parking lot of a log cabin-looking diner that had several other cars in the parking lot. "You go on ahead," Autumn told her friends. "I want to try Zach again."

"Everything okay?" Tiffany asked quietly.

"I hope so," Autumn said. Tiffany nodded and guided the guys into the diner. Autumn dialed Zach's cell number and was relieved when he picked up after two rings.

"Hey, sweetie," he said, and her heart melted. He didn't use terms like that very often, and it usually meant he was either very tired or had been through an emotional event. "How are the mountains?"

"So far I've just been along the trails at the resort," she said. She explained the recent history of the resort. "We ran into two other cryptid hunters who told us about a place called Bigfoot Ridge."

"Bigfoot Ridge? I think I've seen a couple of other places with that name on my travels."

"It's supposedly on the other side of the lake. We're thinking of looking into it tomorrow. So, what are you up to?"

"We got some interesting footage last night," he said.

"And you should see this Boggy Creek monster museum they have in town."

"Oh, Zach." She wished she was with him. "Were you out late last night?"

"Yep." He yawned. "Sorry about that. I have some people to interview today, including a couple of older gentlemen who remember the encounters back about fifty years ago."

"Sounds interesting."

"It is." His voice was warm despite his exhaustion, and she reflected that he seemed to get the same sort of rush from monster investigations that she was starting to feel now that she was here on the peninsula. "From here, we're heading to Kentucky."

"The Pope Lick monster again?" Autumn asked with some trepidation. She knew that had been a troublesome investigation for Zach back in the first season. They hadn't shown it on the episode, but he had confided that he had felt something calling to him, telling him to come out on the train trestle where so many people had met with death. "

"Yep. Hey, maybe this time we'll get bonus footage and the whole country will get to see me freeze in fear."

"Then they'll remember that you're human," she teased. "And you're not the first to have that experience. It lends truth to other stories of the place."

"That's true," he said. "Thanks, Autumn. Keep me updated on what you find out there."

"I'll be in touch when I can," she promised. "Love you, Zach. Be careful out there."

"Love you, too. Don't go anywhere by yourself."

"I promise." She hung up and took a deep breath. Zach had a team to look out for him during his time on the show. She had a team, as well. She got out of the car and went into the diner to join her friends.

CHAPTER 9

When they had finished lunch, Autumn suggested a stroll through the strip of stores next to the diner. Tiffany nodded eagerly. Nate looked at his watch and agreed. Mike, who had been staring out the window for most of the meal, shook his head.

"I'm heading across the highway," he said, pointing to a one-story gray-painted building across the road. "That's a branch of the county library system, and I'm surprised to see it open on a Sunday. I want to see if there are any pictures of the resort from before the closure, or any news articles about the Bobcat Lake Project."

"We'll meet you there," Nate suggested. They paid the bill and left the diner. The misty rain was still hanging around, with the low fog now covering parts of the treetops in the area. Mike waited for a break in the traffic while the others rounded the corner of the diner and found themselves facing a row of ten shops.

"Lots of people here," Tiffany noted as they stepped onto a covered sidewalk and stood out of the rain. "We're not too far from Port Mason and it's a scenic highway. I guess it's a good place to stop to pick up what you might need."

"Convenience store, book store, candy store, gas station on the corner?" Autumn laughed. "Yep, that would be my first place to stock up for a weekend trip in the mountains."

Nate gestured at the bookstore right behind them. "We might as well start here, then."

Thirty minutes later, they returned to the diner and placed their purchases in the car. They waited at the edge of the road until an approaching truck passed, and Autumn saw that the driver was the same park ranger she had seen talking to Jenna. His eyes were on the road ahead of him and he seemed to be talking to someone through his speaker phone.

They entered the library and found Mike at a table on the far side of a comfortable reading room. He was talking to an older man wearing a long-sleeved polo shirt and khakis, and looking at a book. When they approached, Mike looked up and smiled.

"Hey, guys. Andrew, these are my friends, Nate, Autumn, and Tiffany. This is Andrew Baker, the librarian."

"Hello," Andrew said softly with a nod and a smile. "I understand you're curious about Bobcat Lodge."

"We saw an older cabin with fire damage and the remains of a viewing tower when we were on one of the trails this morning," Nate explained. "The owners mentioned that they bought the place after a fire and other mysterious occurrences made the former owners shut down the property for a couple of years."

"We're curious about the fire and what scared the formers owners away," Autumn said. Andrew raised his eyebrows and nodded.

"I imagine Jenna and Donnie probably won't tell you very much about that. They've had a good summer and I'm sure they'd rather just not think about what happened to the former caretaker who lived in the cabin."

"Do you know what happened?" Autumn asked.

Andrew looked around the library. Only a few other patrons were browsing the shelves. Another library employee sat at the checkout desk, looking at something on her phone. He nodded. "Have a seat. I'll be right back." He moved quickly, disappearing around the corner of the desk.

"Look," Mike said, turning the book around and pointing to a picture. The book appeared to be a collection of photos from lodging around the peninsula. "There's the original lodge, which hasn't changed much on the outside. And here's a photo of the caretaker's cabin."

Autumn stared at the familiar building. It looked like it had once been a comfortable place to live, which matched her impression of the items that had been left behind. Nate nodded at the photo, and Tiffany studied it for a moment. "Someone lived there?" she asked.

"Apparently," Nate said. "Let's see what Andrew has to tell us."

The librarian was approaching their table, this time with several books in his hands. One appeared to be a collection of newspaper clippings. The others were thin paperback books. Autumn recognized one of them as being a collection of Bigfoot stories from the state. She had a copy of it on her bookshelf at home.

"I've never been a big believer in monsters like Bigfoot, but I also can't deny that there are a lot of compelling stories out there," Andrew said as he sat down at the table and placed the books in the center, fanning them out so the others could reach for them. "I started my own collection of newspaper clippings about a year before the fire at the resort. It was around the same time that the trail leading up to one of the hot springs sites was washed away."

"People can still visit the hot springs, though, right?" Tiffany asked. "We've heard that it's a popular destination."

Andrew nodded. "Yes. It's quite a hike, though. They put up a wooden footbridge across the washout area that people can use. It's a good five miles or more up to the hot springs, so people make a whole day out of it. There was a period of time when the hot springs had almost no visitors, other than park service employees and contractors working on the flood damage. When people started returning to the hot springs, the rangers started getting reports of people being watched from the forest."

"Watched? By other people?"

"I guess that's always the question, isn't it? Of course, the standard park ranger response is that they saw a bear on its hind legs."

"What about Bobcat Lodge?" Nate interrupted. Mike nudged him, and Nate shrugged. Andrew opened the clippings notebook and turned it around so Nate and Mike could see it. Autumn moved her chair over so she could also look at what had happened. Tiffany pulled a collection of Bigfoot stories to her end of the table and opened it.

"The fire started during the middle of the night, mid-September, somewhere near the caretaker's cabin. Flames spread to the nearby viewing tower, and then winds pushed the fire through the forest over to the last two cabins at that end of the property. Thankfully, no guests were staying in the cabins at the time."

"What about the caretaker's cabin?" Mike asked. "Was someone living there?"

"Yes. A widower named Tate Tyler. He was in his fifties, a retired park ranger, and had taken on the job to stay busy in his retirement. He was found dead about fifty feet away from the cabin. The initial assumption was that an explosion had thrown him through the forest. There were questions about his wounds, though, and not a lot of burns on his body. When his body was found, part of his skull had been crushed and there were tears in his clothes as if a bear had mauled him."

The group winced. "Jenna and Donnie didn't mention that someone had died there," Autumn whispered.

"Bears again," Tiffany muttered.

"We didn't any signs of a massive fire beyond the cabin itself this morning," Nate pointed out. "If it's only been three years since this happened, then the plants grew back fairly quickly."

Andrew shrugged. "Some of the undergrowth is probably still scorched, but yes, that was something that was made a priority. People came in and replanted trees and relocated many other plant species to support the former owners of the property. They wanted the paths on the resort to still be walkable. They cleared the area around the caretaker's cabin in case equipment needed to be brought onto the property. The two cabins that the flames touched were left empty for the next month while the caretakers decided what to do.

"Word had spread that they were just about ready to make some renovations when, to everyone's surprise, the last guests left, and Paul and Lisa Ewing placed a chain across the driveway. Around mid-October, a park ranger visited them to see what happened and discovered that they were hiding in their apartment inside the main lodge. They told him that a large, hairy creature was stalking them, and almost killed Paul when he was out in the forest. He barely escaped by climbing into one of the viewing towers. According to the article that later emerged from the park ranger's visit, the creature let out a roar that almost deafened him and managed to shake the tree hard enough to rattle the tower."

Tiffany put down the book she was reading. Autumn sat back in her chair. Nate and Mike looked at each other, then back at Andrew. "That would have to be a massive creature," Nate said softly.

"The door at the cabin," Autumn added. "We theorized that an explosion blew it off its hinges. Maybe it was the monster. That's probably why Tate Tyler was found so far from the cabin. He tried to run, and the creature followed him."

"Maybe Tate Tyler set the fire to try to escape from the creature," Tiffany added.

Andrew looked at them thoughtfully. "Paul and Lisa also mentioned that there might be more than one of the monsters around the lake. They wanted out of the property, and out of the park. The ranger who had visited them, Jake Tyler, helped them pack what they needed and escorted their car off the property. They came back a couple of times to get business records, and occasionally met with prospective buyers of the property. Finally, about a year ago, the Stalbergs came in and made an offer that that Paul and Lisa accepted. As far as I know, they're permanently living on the other side of the state now."

"Jake Tyler," Nate mused. "Any relation to Tate?"

"His son," Andrew said. "Jake is a very diligent park ranger and makes Bobcat Lodge a regular part of his patrol. If you're interested in looking for Bigfoot, you probably want to make sure you don't run into Jake out in the forest. He's pretty down-to-earth, but also likely to tell you to leave if you're in the wrong place."

Autumn wondered if Jake Tyler was the ranger she had seen with Jenna this morning. "Surely there's more than one park ranger out here," she said. "It's such a vast area."

Andrew nodded. "There's a park ranger substation down at the other end of the lake, where there's a turnoff from Highway to 101 to some of the smaller roads in the area. You'll probably pass it if you're interested in Bigfoot Ridge."

Mike looked startled. "I didn't mention that to you."

"You didn't have to. The Olympic National Park has been a big draw for Bigfoot seekers for many years. There are lots of places where people can take day hikes and claim that a rustling of tree branches and a bad smell equals a Bigfoot sighting. Bigfoot Ridge got that name within the past couple of years, after it was abandoned by the researchers working in the area. That was about six months after the fire."

"What kind of researchers?" Autumn asked.

"The official name is the Bobcat Lake Research Project," Andrew explained. "It's roughly four hundred acres of land surrounded by a fence. A couple of years before the fire, teams of geologists, botanists, and biologists were hired to observe and document the natural resources within that area. They were coming in and out of the property throughout the year. There were plenty of rocks, plants, and animal species to keep them occupied."

"Then what happened?" Nate asked.

"The scientists eventually asked the park rangers to start accompanying them while they were inside the fence. They installed a large metal gate at the entrance with a lock, although all the scientists and the rangers had keys. There's a woman living down the road from Bigfoot Ridge, on Bobcat Lake, who coordinated the whole project, and she was the last person to be inside the area after the scientists left." He shook his head. "I don't know what she saw, but she doesn't talk about it with many people. She was checking on the abandoned project every week until the project grant officially ended a few months ago."

"Do you think we might be able to talk to this woman?" Autumn asked eagerly.

"I don't know. She's a friend of mine, though. How about I call her and ask, and leave a message at the resort for you?"

"Thank you. We'd appreciate that."

"Where is this area, exactly?" Nate asked. "Someone at the resort mentioned the place to us yesterday, and we thought it might be interesting to go and do an investigation with all of our equipment."

Andrew opened up one of the books and turned to a map of Bobcat Lake. He turned the map around to show the group. "When you're leaving the lodge, you turn right instead of left, and follow the highway. When you get to the intersection with the ranger station, turn right, and that will start taking you around the lake. Go past the clearly marked Marmot Trail, and about half a mile down from that, you'll see the gate. I'm not encouraging you to go, mind you. There's a reason that people who live here stay away, and why the scientists abandoned their work. Enter at your own risk."

"Have you directed many people there?" Mike asked, holding down the page with the map.

"There are other people who have been looking for information on Bigfoot and the places where they might have a better chance of finding it. Those people haven't heard the story I just told you, and I didn't offer it to them. Have you encountered someone named Cole Patterson yet?"

"He's staying at the resort for a few days," Tiffany said. "Him and his girlfriend, Laine Dawson."

"Laine is very intelligent, and I'm guessing she's probably been up here so much because her employer is looking to expand operations and maybe build another hotel in Port Mason," Andrew said. "That's what I gather from the conversations I've had with her when she and Cole have come in to do some research."

"And what about Cole?" Autumn said. "I know he's self-published a lot of cryptid stories. Other than that, he didn't come across as doing much besides trying to get internet-famous for looking for Bigfoot."

"There are a lot of shows with that type of thing," Andrew said. "Have you ever heard of *Creature Hunt*? I may be pretty skeptical about creatures like Bigfoot, but the host of that show is very fun to watch."

Autumn smiled and looked around at her friends. "Yes, we know the show."

"Anyway, I wouldn't worry too much about Cole. He may get up to some pranks to try to stir some attention, but for the most part he just likes to write stories about other people's encounters. I guess that's how he makes most of his money."

Andrew looked up at the clock, then at the small group of people that had just entered the building. "Excuse me, I need to speak with these people. Feel free to look through all of these books and bring them back to the checkout desk when you're done."

"Can we check out this book, with the map?" Mike asked.

"No, it's a reference book only. Feel free to make copies of anything you need, though. Have a nice day." He smiled and retreated to the library entrance.

"This sounds promising," Tiffany said, looking at the book she had been reading. "The chapter is actually titled 'Encounter near the Hot Springs.'" She leaned in closer and read out loud. "I saw several older picnic tables and thought it would be a good place to sit and look out over the river. Just before I sat down, I smelled an incredibly nasty stench, as if a dead animal was nearby. I had second thoughts and turned around to go back to my car. Out of the corner of my eye, I thought I saw a large figure retreat behind a tree. I hurried out of there. I didn't want to see the source of that smell."

"Well, I think we're all pretty much agreed that Bigfoot Ridge is our next step," Autumn said. "When do we want to go?"

"Tomorrow," Nate said firmly. "I don't want to take a chance on getting stuck in the forest at night out here, and our equipment is back at the cabin."

"I'll go make copies of the map," Mike said. "And I think we should talk to Jenna and Donnie if we can, to see what else they might know about Tate Tyler and the cabin."

"I'd rather hold off on that," Autumn said. "I don't think they'd be really open to discussing it, especially if they think we're trying to connect it to Bigfoot."

Nate pointed to Tiffany's book. "Is there anything about Batsquatch in there?"

She scanned the chapter titles. "No. I think Laine and Cole are just making that up."

"What about a dogman?"

"Not that, either."

"Hoaxes," Nate snorted. "Just what we're looking for, right?"

"Let's finish up and go," Autumn suggested. "We have to prepare for tomorrow." Her friends agreed. They made copies and returned the books. As they left, Autumn noticed Andrew studying them while the group he was leading around the library went into the reference room. He waved, and she waved back. She was disturbed by the death at the resort, but also even more curious about the monster that had scared away the previous owners. She was glad they had found some answers, and hoped that soon she'd be able to find some evidence of Bigfoot.

CHAPTER 10

On the way back to Bobcat Lodge, Autumn watched the scenery as she listened to Nate and Tiffany talking about what they had learned at the library. Mike seemed lost in his own thoughts. He slowed down to let two deer run across the highway. They ran swiftly, and one of the deer stopped to look behind him, as if waiting for another animal to follow. Autumn sat up and looked down what appeared to be an old logging road on the other side of the highway. Was that really a large, bipedal animal she had just seen?

"Turn around!" she demanded. "Mike, turn around. I saw something in the forest back there."

Mike slammed on his brakes and the SUV came to a stop on the side of the road. "What the hell, Autumn?" Nate asked, turning around to look at her. "What did you see?"

"I think it was the creature those deer were running from," she said quietly, calmer now that the car was stopped. "Please, Mike. Turn around and pull up by that old logging road back there."

"Alright," he sighed. He checked for traffic and let two cars pass, then swung out onto the pavement and turned the car in the other direction.

"Do we have anything in here that might hold some sort of evidence, like hair or blood? Any containers?" Autumn asked. Tiffany, sitting next to her in the backseat, turned around to look at the cargo area.

"I don't think so," she said, rummaging through a box. "Oh, wait. Here are some plastic bags."

"Better than nothing." Autumn took the bags from her. "Is everything else back at the cabin, Mike?"

"Yes. I didn't want to leave it in the car while it was sitting in the parking lot." He slowed again and stopped at the chain that blocked the road. "Is this the place?"

"Yes."

They all studied the signs that warned that they were entering National Park Service property and that trespassers would be prosecuted. Autumn thought that the road, which she was still assuming had been used for logging operations, had been shut down years ago. It looked like no trucks had come through here for quite some time. There was a line of plants growing up through the gravel in the middle of the road, and no tire tracks were visible in the dirt either on their side of the chain or on the road that disappeared into the forest.

"Okay," Mike said, turning off the engine and taking his keys out of the ignition. "Let's go for a hike."

"Should someone stay here?" Tiffany asked.

"I think the car will be okay," Nate said. He opened the door and stepped out, stretching his arms. He checked his watch. "It's almost four o'clock. How about we agree to only stay out here for an hour? We don't want to get so far away from the highway that we can't find our way back."

"Unlikely we'd get that lost," Tiffany said. She zipped up her jacket and also got out of the car. The sun had emerged while they had been in the library, although the clouds were still present. "Okay, let's check out what Autumn thought she saw."

"What I saw," Autumn corrected her as she got out of the car and closed the door. Two passenger vehicles and a commercial truck went by on the highway, not bothering to slow down as they passed the group on the side of the road. "I've got the plastic bags. Do we need anything else?"

"We all have our phones, right? We can take pictures and upload them to the laptop later. Everything else is back at the cabin. So, let's get going," Mike said.

They walked to the chain blocking the road and lifted it up to walk under it, as it was placed slightly too high for them to climb over the barrier. Staying close together, they kept to the center of the road and walked forward. Autumn kept her eyes ahead of her, looking for the possible spot where the creature had crossed this road and entered the forest. Tiffany kept looking back over her shoulder, as if waiting for a park ranger to appear and order them back to the safety of the car.

"Hey, look there," Nate said, pointing to a muddy area at the edge of the gravel. They gathered around it and found two deep impressions on the ground, along with a tree that had a dark stain on the side of the trunk. "Footprints?" he asked Mike.

"Maybe." Mike took some photos, as did Nate. Autumn looked at the stain on the tree, but shook her head. "I think it's just pitch or something," she said. "It's not blood, or at least not fresh blood."

Tiffany shivered, and Nate rubbed her back. Just beyond the mud, Autumn could see that several bushes had been flattened and downed tree limbs shoved aside, forming a winding path through the forest. "Hey, let's follow that," she said, pointing to the path. She led the way, and the group followed.

Twenty minutes of walking through the forest began to make Autumn wonder if she really had seen something. The path that had been created by a large animal moving across the dense underbrush came to a stop right at a clearing. She stood still and looked around, noticing that her friends were several steps behind her. She listened, and noticed that the forest was silent. No birds singing, no squirrels chattering, nothing moved through the plants. Everything was silent.

A chill ran down her spine. She turned around and saw that Tiffany was pointing to something beside a tree, her mouth turned down in disgust. Autumn walked back to join them and saw a deer carcass. Its abdomen had been ripped open and claw marks were visible leading to the wound. *Claw marks?* Autumn questioned silently. Were they looking for a Bigfoot, or the more sinister dogman? She hadn't expected to see more signs of the bipedal canine here.

Nate kneeled down and put a hand against the deer's neck, well away from the guts that were spilled out across the dirt. "It's still warm," he breathed.

Mike, who had been taking lots of pictures, suddenly stopped and sniffed. "Do you smell that?"

"A rotting corpse?" Tiffany hissed. "Yes. Let's get out of here, please."

Nate backed away from the deer. "Oh, man. That's not the deer."

A low, growling sound made all of them look back into the clearing. Autumn thought she saw something duck back behind a tree. It was large, and wide, and covered with hair. "Hey!" she shouted. Nate shushed her.

"I agree with Tiffany," he said. "Let's get out of here."

"Let me get cut a piece from around the deer's wound," Autumn insisted. "Maybe there's some saliva or something." She pulled out her pocketknife and bent down. Cutting into dead animals was not something she had ever enjoyed, but here was a chance to maybe get some Bigfoot DNA samples.

Just as she opened the knife, a loud roar startled her and the others. She dropped the knife and swore, then hastily picked it up, folding the blade back into the handle. She backed away from the deer and saw that Mike and Nate both had their phones up in the direction of the creature hiding behind the tree.

"Let's go," Tiffany urged again. Autumn looked down at the deer again and nodded. There was probably going to be a dispute between several animals in these woods over the deer carcass. This was no time to be interrupting even a known animal like a bear. They were standing between that creature and its food source, and it was undoubtedly still hungry.

"Okay," Nate said. He and Mike put away their phones. Mike led the way out through the trail they had followed on the way to the clearing.

As they walked back to the road, Autumn could hear tree

limbs and bushes moving behind and around them. At one point, it seemed the creature had already caught up to them because they could hear heavy breathing. No bear or coyote or large cat would stalk the group like this, Autumn reasoned. They had made sufficient noise on the way in for those creatures to shy away until they were gone. Every time she looked off into the forest, she caught nothing more than glimpses of dark fur and a large shape.

They reached the logging road and were headed back to the SUV when Tiffany suddenly stumbled as a rock hit her left leg. She fell over a large tree root and landed face-down on the gravel. She screamed in pain, and Nate bent down to check on her. "My ankle hurts," she whimpered, sitting up and reaching for her foot.

"Can you stand up?" Mike asked quietly. "Because I think whatever threw that rock is losing patience with us being here." Just as he said that, another rock came sailing right at Autumn. She saw it just in time to duck, then lost her balance and hit the ground. The gravel dug into her arms. When she sat up, she noticed a couple of bloody scrapes.

"I think it's a Bigfoot," she said. "What other animal could have the ability to throw rocks?"

"A human," Nate said grimly. "Trying to scare us away from something hidden out here."

A roar broke through their concentration. Another rock sailed past them, this one almost the size of Nate's head. He backed away and nearly fell over Tiffany. "Forget that," he said. "Let's get out of here."

"Please," Tiffany said. Nate helped her up, and he and Mike helped her walk down the trail, staying to one side of the road that had more even terrain. Autumn, still sitting on the ground, turned to face the forest.

"We're leaving!" she called out. A tree limb, almost four inches around, sailed over her head. She scrambled along the ground until she found her footing, and stood. She walked quickly to catch up with the others. Just as they reached the chain and the highway, they noticed that they could hear forest sounds again and the rotting flesh smell was gone.

"I think we're okay," Autumn breathed.

"Maybe safe from the Bigfoot," Mike said. "But here's a new bit of trouble."

A National Park Service truck was pulled up behind Mike's vehicle. Autumn recognized the man standing near the SUV. He was a little over six feet tall, with brown hair and dark eyes. He was wearing a park ranger uniform. His arms were crossed and he leaned casually against his truck as he watched the group walking to the vehicle. Tiffany was limping now, and Mike opened the passenger door so that she could sit down.

"Hi. I'm Ranger Jake Tyler. I'm with the National Park Service. Having car trouble?" the ranger asked. Up close, Autumn could see that his eyes were actually dark green, and he looked like he hadn't shaved in a few days.

"No," Mike said. "We thought we saw…"

Autumn stepped in. "Hi, Ranger Tyler. I'm Autumn Hunter." She introduced the rest of the group. "We stopped when we saw some deer crossing the road earlier and wondered if maybe there would be a good place to go hiking down this trail."

"So, you just wandered past the 'No Trespassing' and other signs?" Ranger Tyler asked. "There are plenty of other places to hike within the park. You should go explore some of them. Hurricane Ridge is nice this time of year."

"I'm sure it is," Autumn said. "I think I already saw you earlier today, at Bobcat Lodge. That's where we're staying. You were talking with one of the owners, Jenna Stalberg."

"Yes," he said. "They're friends of mine, and the lodge is part of my regular patrol." He uncrossed his arms and walked over to Tiffany. "Are you injured, ma'am?"

"I tripped over some tree roots," Tiffany said. "They just

seemed to come out of nowhere."

He looked at Autumn's arms. "Did you trip, too?"

"Yes," she replied. She couldn't quite meet his intense gaze, though, and thought that he didn't believe their stories.

"I thought I heard some shouting before you got back to the car," Ranger Tyler said. "Anyone want to change their story?"

Nate closed the passenger door and let Tiffany relax in the front seat. "Okay, Ranger Tyler. You want the truth? We were back there because Autumn thought she saw a large animal crossing the logging road. We're here to look for Bigfoot."

Ranger Tyler was silent for several minutes, long enough for Nate to start shuffling his feet. Autumn's arms were starting to sting, so she opened the rear passenger door and reached in for her purse. She pulled out some alcohol wipes and wiped down the scrapes, then put the wipes into a plastic bag to throw out later. She'd cover them with a bandage back at the cabin.

"Okay, here's all I can tell you. Stay away from unmarked trails, and follow whatever precautions you'd take while hiking. Make sure you have bear spray if you're going deep into the forest, and that someone knows where you are and can contact us if there's a problem." Ranger Tyler backed away from them and got back into his truck. He started the engine and sat in his seat, continuing to watch the group.

"I guess he wants us to leave first," Nate said. "Let's go."

Mike eagerly got behind the wheel. They made a left turn onto the highway and headed back to the resort. Autumn wondered if any useful photos were on Mike's phone, and she also thought about the park ranger. He seemed resigned to their mission, and had given them the standard information they'd need for any forest exploration. She believed that he knew more about what they had seen on that road than he was willing to admit.

CHAPTER 11

Faye Carson hung up her phone. Her hand had started shaking when Andrew Baker brought up Bigfoot Ridge, and asked her if she'd be willing to talk to a group of people who had come in to the library this afternoon. "I know you've been hassled by Cole Patterson before, Faye. For what's it worth, I think these people are seeking out solid proof of Bigfoot."

"The Bobcat Lake Project is shut down, locked, and off-limits to the public," she had told him flatly. "They shouldn't be seeking anything there."

"You and I both know that hasn't stopped people in the past. Are you willing to talk to them?"

"Maybe," she had surprised herself by saying. "They're staying over at Bobcat Lodge?"

"Yes."

"I may just go over there and surprise them. Do you have any names?"

He had given her Autumn and Nate's names. "I'll ask Jenna to let me know how to locate them if I go over there," she said. "Thanks for calling, Andrew."

"I didn't mean to upset you."

"I know. Really, I'm not upset. I just wish all of this would die down instead of being continually stirred up. Talk to you later."

"Have a good day, Faye."

She sat down in her living room. When the National Park Service had decided that the four hundred acres between the Marmot Trail and the residences along the northern shore of Bobcat Lake would be a perfect spot to set up an enclosed wildlife research area, she had applied for the job of project manager. Before moving out to the peninsula permanently to settle down in her family's cabin, she had managed similar programs in other areas of the state. It had come naturally to her when she had graduated with a degree in biology and a minor in business, and she had made an almost thirty-year career out of being in forests and fields, keeping people on task with their assigned studies of the plants and animals throughout Washington.

The first three years of the Bobcat Lake Project, as they had always referred to it, had gone well. The scientists were already talking about getting their grants extended past the initial five-year period. There had been plenty of time off for Faye, as the researchers would come up and stay for a couple of weeks at a time while they gathered their data, and then go back to their labs or offices and work on other projects.

In the middle of August, almost three years ago, one of the biologists, Ray, had approached Faye and asked her to look at something disturbing. She had been expecting to see dead animals or that the makeshift office had been disturbed by trespassers. Instead, she had been shown a large footprint. It was nearly eighteen inches long and had a clear outline of toes at the front of the foot. "This is the only one I've seen," Ray had told her, his voice unsteady. "Does this look like a bear track to you?"

Her first instinct had been to tell him that yes, it was a bear track. She couldn't bring herself to do that, though. Instead, she had shook her head and asked him what he was going to do with the footprint. "Document it, and get a cast," he had told her. "Then I'm going to keep an eye out at all times for whatever is walking around in here with feet that large."

Faye had settled down into her usual chair underneath the tent that had been set up to keep the testing equipment out of the elements. She had seen footprints that large before in the Cascades, but had never encountered the legendary monster that supposedly inhabited the forests of the state. She had never seen a Bigfoot.

Still, she thought it best to be safe and had contacted the park service. She had spoken to the Chief Ranger for Olympic National Park and had requested that during the weeks when the project site was open, he assign one of the law enforcement rangers to be on site. He had questioned the need for such an action, but reluctantly agreed.

Her neighbor, Jake Tyler, was the ranger on duty at the project area a few times, and she had felt reassured by his presence. Even after Tate had died in that fire, she knew that Jake was still on the job and ready to act if needed. He had usually stayed in his truck by the gate, seldom venturing deeper down the path to where the researchers did most of their experiments.

During the fall, Bob, a geologist, had mentioned finding a small cave near the cliff at the back edge of the property. There had been branches and leaves in there that appeared to have been a nest for what he called "a very large animal. Maybe a bear, but we haven't seen any bears inside the fence for at least a year and there was a fresh smell inside the cave. A really rotten one. I had to step outside several times while I was taking pictures and getting samples from the cave entrance."

Then, Angie, one of the botanists, had come across a patch of trees with several limbs torn off. "Torn," she had emphasized. "Not cut. I realize that a chain link fence isn't going to keep people out of they really want to trespass in here, but I don't see why even pranksters would climb over the fence, walk several acres into the forest, and then tear down tree limbs. I'm not sure even two or three people could do it. And the limbs were fairly high up for people to reach without a ladder. Maybe eight or nine feet off the ground."

It was in April that everything had come to a head. One morning, while Jake was on duty, Faye had decided to take a walk through the project area. It was a cool spring morning, sunny, and she had just watched as Ray, Angie, and Bill had gathered up their notebooks and cameras and headed out to the various corners of the acreage. She was expecting a calm day, as there were only two more days of everyone being on site for this cycle.

A scream had stopped her in her tracks, making her blood run cold. She had turned around, looking in all directions, trying to figure out where the sound had come from. Then, another scream, followed by a shout, pointed her in the direction of Bob's cave site. She started running, wondering if Jake had also figured out where to go. He had his truck and could probably get there quicker than she could.

She emerged into a clearing and stopped. Bob and Angie were on the other side, staring with awe and horror at a creature standing with its back to her. She saw that it was probably between nine and ten feet tall, over seven hundred pounds, with muscles that were clearly defined under the long brown hair that covered its body. Its arms hung down far longer than any human arms would go, and its massive hands were starting to curl into fists. She saw the conical shape of its head, and instantly recognized the creature from so many descriptions she had heard and read over the years. It was a Bigfoot, here in the project site.

"Oh, no," Angie moaned. "No. This isn't real."

The creature started growling. It shuffled around so that it was nearly facing all of them, although Faye couldn't see its features. Ray suddenly appeared behind Bob. "Oh my God," he said. "Is that...?" his voice trailed away as the creature bent and picked up a rock.

"Hey!" someone shouted, and Faye had recognized Jake's voice. "Ranger Tyler here! Is someone in danger?"

The Bigfoot turned, and Faye was startled by its eyes. She had expected the eyes and face of a monster, but these were almost human eyes. The face was that of an ape, but a larger ape than she had ever seen. The creature looked around at all of them again, then dropped the rock and ran away into the forest with surprisingly swift steps. Faye watched it leave, unable to move. Only a few seconds later, Jake ran up to her, almost out of breath.

"What happened?" he asked. He looked around and the clearing and grimaced. "What is that smell? And what was walking around through here?" He pointed to the few tracks that were visible.

Angie started sobbing. Bob put an arm around her and shook his head. "I guess a bear finally made it back through the fence somewhere," he said pointedly, staring at Faye. "I think we should finish up whatever we need to do today and leave a couple of days early."

Ray cleared his throat. "Yep, definitely a black bear. Sort of surprising, actually. It was up on its hind legs when I got here. It was probably more surprised than we were." He shook his head and turned, leaving the area with a pace that didn't surprise Faye. If she could, she'd run away right now too.

"I never want to see that again," Angie said. She and Bob left the clearing. Angie walked unsteadily, leaning on Bob. Jake stared at Faye.

"She's that upset over a bear? Did none of you have any bear spray?"

It was only then that Faye remembered she had left hers in the tent. It probably would have warded off the creature had it tried to attack them. She vowed that she'd never go in the forest without protection again. "It sort of snuck up on her, I guess," she finally told Jake. "When you get used to not seeing large animals around, it can be a shock when one shows up."

"You know, I noticed that. Even with the fence up, you'd think coyotes or bobcats could get in here. The area at the edge of the cliff has enough room for them to get around. But Ray told me that he's only seen the smaller mammals in here recently."

Faye shrugged. It was all she could do. She had no explanation for any of it. "Maybe the wildlife didn't like being studied." Jake had given her an odd smile, but didn't say much as he walked her back to his truck. He had driven her to the tent, where she waited the rest of the day for everyone to bring their results back in from the field. There were no more sightings that day of the creature and they had indeed closed the project down early.

That had been the last time any of the scientists had come out to the peninsula, as far as Faye knew. They had all been paid for the rest of the project since they had produced their required studies, and she had been paid to keep an eye on the project property. The grant had ended this summer, and she had not set foot near that area in several months.

This past spring, a writer named Cole Patterson had started coming down to the cottages. This was a close-knit community of about fifty people, most of them having had parents and grandparents who had owned their cabins before them. Cole and his girlfriend, Laine, had been asking about the project area, saying that people had started to call the area Bigfoot Ridge because they claimed to have seen evidence of the creature there.

Faye was skeptical of that claim, since she knew that the rangers regularly drove by the project site and encouraged anyone who might be asking about it to go hiking on the Marmot Trail, located next to the western edge of the area. She doubted that many people had actually dared to go over the gate and into the project area. If anyone did, they probably didn't encounter the creature. She and her team had been working there for nearly three years before they had caught sight of Bigfoot. It knew how to stay away from people, and she had a sense it only wanted to defend its territory and live peacefully on its own.

Faye and other neighbors had complained to Jake, and he had talked to Cole and Laine, telling them that they would be arrested for trespassing if they were found on one of the cottage properties again. Faye had looked up Cole online and read some of the stories that had been sent to him on his website. Some seemed completely made up. There were also some that were eerily similar to her encounter. Those were the ones that had made her shiver.

She also felt that there was something else out in the woods near here. She had heard a howling sound the other night, at first coming from the other side of the lake, then, a few hours later, it had sounded closer to her cabin. She had looked out and seen nothing, but the next morning there had been some claw marks on a tree near her dock.

Last night, she had heard something walking around her

cabin. When she got out of bed to see what it was, she had then also heard what sounded like nails or claws against the side of the building. She had almost called Jake, but then the sound had stopped. When she had gathered up to the courage to look out the window near the front door, she had seen a large canine creature slinking away from her property. It had dark fur, and when it had turned back to look at the cabin, she had seen glowing yellow eyes.

She didn't want to think about another monster that could be stalking the woods of the peninsula, but she wondered if somehow wolves had been set loose in the park without anyone telling the public. That was the only explanation she could think of for the size of the creature she had seen. She had heard about upright-walking canine creatures that supposedly roamed around somewhere out in the Midwest, but she had never heard about any in Washington.

She considered Andrew's request. He was a pretty good judge of character, and had been gracious about keeping the library open late for the scientists of the Bobcat Lake project. It wouldn't hurt to go talk to this woman, Autumn, and her friends and see what they expected to find at the place now called Bigfoot Ridge.

CHAPTER 12

Mike pulled into a parking spot at Bobcat Lodge and turned around. "I think there's a first aid office in the lodge. Do either of you need to go there?"

Autumn looked down at her arms. "I could probably use some bandages for these scrapes."

Tiffany opened her door and stepped out. Nate followed her and held her hand as she took a couple of steps. She shook her head. "I think it's just a mild sprain. I probably just need to put it up with some ice and ibuprofen, and I'll be okay. The tree root did more damage than the rock."

"It can't hurt to at least look at your leg," Nate urged her. She hesitated, then nodded acceptance.

Autumn got out of the car and followed the others into the lodge. Jenna was near the gift shop, talking to a couple of employees. She saw them come in the door and gasped. "Autumn! Tiffany! Are you okay?"

"Just a couple of mishaps on a trail," Autumn replied. "Do you have a place where we can get some bandages?"

"Of course." Jenna motioned for them to follow her down the hall. "Laine and Cole were asking if we had seen you just a few minutes ago. I think they're eating out tonight."

A glance at the clock on the wall told Autumn that it was after five and the dining room was open. "I'm sure we'll probably see them somewhere around the resort tonight."

Jenna opened the door to a comfortable lounge. Just beyond the lounge, an open door led to a medical exam room lined with glass-fronted shelves displaying medical supplies. "Sarah?" she called out.

A tall, thin woman wearing medical scrubs appeared in the exam room's doorway. "Hi, Mom. I see we have some injured guests."

"I'll leave them with you," Jenna said. She smiled and closed the door behind her.

Sarah motioned for Tiffany to follow her into the exam room. Everyone followed, and Sarah seemed ready to ask if they would wait in the other room before Nate explained that he was Tiffany's boyfriend. "And Autumn has scrapes on her arms, so she needs some help, too."

Nate and Mike helped Tiffany up onto the exam table, Sarah pulled up her pants leg. Autumn gasped at the sight of the swollen ankle and large bruise forming above it. "Oh, dear," Nate murmured.

"I'll be in the waiting area," Mike said. He pulled out his phone and closed the door behind him.

"I'll wrap up your ankle with an elastic bandage. Do you have some ibuprofen?" Sarah asked after feeling around the ankle and asking Tiffany questions about how she had injured it.

Tiffany nodded. "I always have some with me."

Sarah finished with Tiffany and turned to Autumn, looking at the shallow wounds. "Gravel?" she asked, pulling out a piece of rock that Autumn had missed. "Not many trails with gravel around here." She wiped both arms again with alcohol and applied gauze pads to the area with tape. When she had finished with both women, Nate helped Tiffany off the table. She tested her weight on the ankle for a few steps and nodded.

"You're Jenna and Donnie's daughter?" Mike asked Sarah.

"Yep. I work here part-time and I'm also a nurse over in Port Mason. Most guests here either end up with insect stings or sunburn. Any major injuries get sent over to the city."

"Has anyone ever claimed they were attacked by an animal here?" he asked.

"On the property? Not likely. Animals tend to avoid noisy areas, and the summer can get probably loud around here. Actually, the fall weekends have been pretty noisy, as well. People were happy that this place finally opened again." Sarah gave them a thin smile. "Let me know if you need anything else."

She sent them away with a small bag of extra bandages and a paper about ankle sprains for Tiffany. "Let's get dinner as long as we're in the lodge," Nate suggested. "We can talk later about what happened today."

"Good. I'm hungry," Mike said. Tiffany nodded, and they entered the dining room. Autumn was glad for the chance to site back, relax, and refuel before discussing the next part of their investigation.

"After this afternoon, I'm even more interested in looking at Bigfoot Ridge," Nate said when they had retreated to the library after dinner. Autumn examined the map of the lake and found the road that Andrew had described to them this afternoon.

"There's no way we would want to hike over there even though there's a way through to the road along the lake shore," she said, tracing a line around the lake with her finger. "Not with all the equipment we'll need."

"There's no way," Mike agreed. "Even without the equipment, that's a long hike."

"We're bringing the laptop and the speakers, right?" Nate said calmly. "We'll have to pack them in the SUV in the morning."

"I still want to come along with you," Tiffany said, her leg propped up on one of the chairs across from her. "I can do my usual thing in the car. Thankfully, it's not going to be too cold tomorrow."

Autumn looked at the weather forecast on the wall. "It's going to be sunny and in the mid-fifties. If you want to be our point person again, you'd probably be fine in the car. And you can keep your foot elevated."

"Have any of you ever heard of this Bigfoot Ridge on the BOG forum?" Mike asked. He had retreated to the computer and logged in to the forum. He was looking through the website, having searched for any mention of the place. "A keyword search doesn't pull up any results."

"Andrew said the name was the Bobcat Lake Research Project," Tiffany said. "Bigfoot Ridge probably just gets passed along by word of mouth."

"Hey, here's an update from a post on Friday. Someone's claiming that they were near the cliff by the Marmot Trail and saw a wounded cougar being stalked by a wolf in the valley below, about fifty feet down and across the field. The wolf was walking on two legs."

"A dogman?" Autumn wondered quietly.

"Or they misjudged the size of a Bigfoot," Nate countered. "How good of a view could they have gotten from that high above the field?"

"Here's a comment about how the hot springs attract Bigfoot, especially during the fall and winter." Mike leaned in closer to the screen. "Patterson520. Any bets on that being Cole's user name?"

"He didn't mention being a member of the BOG forum," Autumn said.

"Looks like this is the area we want to explore," Nate said, joining Autumn at the map. He pointed to the small oblong area of the map that was shaded in dark green and outlined with a thick line, indicating a fence of some sort. "We'll need to go past the ranger station. Do you think we should check in with Ranger Tyler to let him know we'll be in the area?"

"Let's decide that tomorrow," Mike said.

Autumn looked at where Nate's finger had landed. It fit Andrew's description of the research area. She wondered why the area had been abandoned and wished they could speak to the woman Andrew had mentioned to them. She would have bet almost anything that there had been a Bigfoot encounter.

"Good thing I brought a lot of books," Tiffany laughed, lightly limping over to them and putting an arm around Nate. He hugged her. Given what Tiffany had experienced this afternoon, Autumn was surprised that Tiffany wasn't just going to stay behind at the cabin.

"Let's leave here around nine," Mike suggested. He logged off the computer and stretched.

Cole Patterson appeared in the doorway, as if he had been

waiting in the hallway, listening to their discussion. "It's the intrepid Bigfoot hunters. Found anything yet?"

Autumn crossed her arms and opened her mouth, but Mike sent her a warning glance. "Not yet, but we've only had one full day here together. We did some more research after our hikes today, so tomorrow it's time to get and see more around the lake."

"We hear you and Laine were looking for us," Autumn said. "Was there anything you needed to talk to us about?"

"Nope. Laine heard some howls last night. Did you hear anything?"

"I was out cold," Autumn said. "I think everybody else was, too." Her friends, sensing her distrust in Cole, nodded in unison.

"Good luck. Hope you find Bigfoot Ridge."

"Hey, have you actually been in there?" Nate asked.

"No. I've only seen it from the outside."

"And that's as far as you should go," a woman's voice interrupted. Everyone turned to see a gray-haired woman in the doorway. She wore khaki pants and a polo shirt, and was deeply tanned. She had the look of someone who spent a lot of time outdoors.

"Faye," Cole said, backing away from the others. "It's nice to see you again."

"I'm surprised you've managed to stay away from my neighborhood on this trip, Cole."

He smiled weakly. "Some orders from the park rangers are easy to ignore. Others are not."

The woman turned to look at the group. "Is one of you Autumn Hunter?"

Autumn nodded and stepped forward. "That's me."

"I'd like to speak with you and your friends." She glared at Cole. "In private."

He held up his hands and walked to the door. "I have something I need to do, anyway. Good night."

He left, and the woman closed the door behind him. "I'm Faye Carson," she told the group. "Andrew Baker told me that you are interested in Bigfoot Ridge."

"We've been trying for years to get proof of Bigfoot that can lead scientists to finally acknowledge its existence," Autumn said. "We've gathered bits and pieces over the last couple of years, but nothing definitive."

"And encountered some cover-ups," Mike added quietly.

"What happened that made the scientists leave the research area?" Nate asked.

"The official name for those four hundred acres of forest is the Bobcat Lake Research Project. It was designed for a group of biologists, botanists, and geologists to be able to study samples from their respective fields in a mostly contained environment. There were some parts of the property where animals could get in and out, but the fence we built contained most of the animals that were living there." She sat down on the edge of a table. "When the project had been going for a couple of years, we noticed that there seemed to be fewer animals, especially the smaller mammals. A bear that had been seen at the edge of the property was gone. The coyotes and cats that had come through the project area were not being seen anymore, even on the overnight cameras that were set up to catch nocturnal activities."

"Something was hunting them?" Nate asked.

"Or scaring them away. We found a small cave that had become a home for a large animal long after the bear was gone. We also found signs of plants and trees being torn apart or trampled." She paused, and clasped her hands together. "The project ended the day several of us saw a creature inside the project area that we weren't expecting. It was large, and ape-like. It was an encounter that still plays in my mind."

"Was it a Bigfoot?" Autumn asked gently, standing more closely to Faye. She could see Faye's lips trembling.

"I'd never seen one before, in all my years in the field. I had pretty much believed they didn't exist. The only sign of violence happened when an additional person arrived at the clearing where the encounter took place, and the creature picked up a rock."

Autumn glanced at her friends. "Did it throw the rock?"

"No. Ranger Jake Tyler, who was our guard for that day, started shouting and the creature ran away. It was large, and fast. We could feel the ground shake a bit."

"Did Ranger Tyler see the creature?" Autumn asked.

"No. I'm fairly certain of that. We immediately told him we had seen a bear, and it had gone up on its hind legs and scared Angie, the botanist. He believed us."

"And then the project shut down?"

Faye nodded. "No one wanted to return there. I checked it out every week until my contract ended a few months ago, and I haven't gone in there since." She shook her head. "I drove past it on my way here, and saw that some smartass actually painted the name Bigfoot Ridge on the sign."

"Maybe Cole?" Tiffany suggested.

Faye's mouth twisted down. "He was bothering people in my neighborhood earlier this year, trying to get us to talk about the creature. I know some of my neighbors have probably seen it. We've all been here for years, and no one wanted any publicity. Jake lives next door to me, and he warned Cole to stay away from us."

"It seems his warning didn't have much effect on Cole's fascination with Bigfoot Ridge. He just claimed to never have been inside. I wonder why."

"He makes his living sharing other people's stories," Faye said. "I'm surprised that he hasn't already gone in to the property. The gate is always locked, but there are ways around it."

"Do you think the creature is still there?" Autumn asked.

Faye shrugged. "I don't know, and I'd rather not find out. I suggest you go someplace else in the park. The hot springs are nice."

Tiffany laughed. "Everyone keeps bringing those up. I guess we'll have to check them out on a future trip since we need to leave on Tuesday."

"Good luck, whatever your decision," Faye said. She

abruptly opened the door and left the room. Everyone looked at each other in silence.

"Is it wrong that I'm even more excited about what we could find at Bigfoot Ridge?" Autumn asked.

"I believe her story," Nate admitted. "She said others witnessed it, and the fact that they never returned points to them knowing what they saw and not wanting to put themselves in danger."

"I don't think there's much point in discussing it more tonight," Mike said. "We know we're going there, and we'll make sure we're prepared for any animal we'll encounter."

"I'm ready for bed," Autumn announced. "I also need to update my journal."

"Let's hope tomorrow is as eventful as today," Nate said.

They left the library and waved at the receptionist on their way out of the lodge. The night air was chilly, and Autumn hurriedly put on her jacket and zipped it up. She debated wearing gloves, but it was a fairly short walk to the cabin.

The paths were well-lit, and the ground-mounted lights were partially reflected in the lake. Autumn had noticed a "polar bear" swim scheduled for Tuesday morning and shook her head at the thought. Mike kept looking off to the side as they walked. He slowed his pace and so did Autumn, letting Nate and Tiffany walk ahead of them. "You might want to stay up for awhile after everyone else goes to bed tonight," he said softly. "I don't know if Nate and Tiffany saw anything, but last night I got up in the middle of the night to get a drink of water at the sink. When I looked out the window, I saw a pair of glowing red eyes up in the trees."

"The same ones I saw?" Autumn asked quietly.

"Most likely. Probably twenty feet off the ground. Scared the crap out of me, but of course I didn't want to admit that." He grinned ruefully. "I just retreated back to my bedroom. You might have a better view from the loft."

"Thanks," she said. "I have an idea that Laine and Cole are up to something. I just wish I knew what it was."

CHAPTER 13

"Come on, Laine. If the Batsquatch is going to be seen tonight, we need to hustle out to the tower."

Laine looked at her watch and yawned. It was after ten o'clock, and she was tired. When she had first met Cole a few years ago, he was a writer looking to become famous. Since he interviewed people throughout the country and collected stories of monsters, ghosts, and anything odd that people encountered, she had figured that he was well on his way there.

Six months ago, she had learned that her bosses were interested in expanding hotel operations into the northern coast of the peninsula. Laine had always figured that the best place for such a move would be Port Mason, and she had agreed to make several trips to the area around Bobcat Lake and see what the city and the national park could offer their guests. At the main hotel, they were right on the beach, where guests could stroll and play in the sand and surf.

Up here, the terrain along the water was rocky, and the water was rough with high waves. She had figured out that the main selling point was the outdoor offerings in Olympic National Park, with hiking and skiing areas not far away, and the proximity of a small city with lots of amenities for the guests. She had just finished her final report this afternoon, and had been looking forward to an evening of relaxation and quiet time with Cole.

On their first visit here, in the spring, he had insisted on bringing Laine over to the closed-off area that had once housed the Bobcat Lake Project. Laine had actually heard about it a couple of years ago, when one of the geologists working there had stayed on the coast for a weekend vacation before heading back to his job in Seattle. It had surprised her to hear that the project had been shut down, and Cole's story of a Bigfoot roaming the land had made her roll her eyes. He seemed to think that there could be monsters in almost every place they traveled.

When she had gone with him to ask the lakeshore residents about Bigfoot stories, she had been surprised at the cold reception he had received. In most places, people were willing to finally talk about what they had seen to someone who might believe them, and Cole anonymously published their encounters. This time, everyone had declared that even if they had ever seen something that could be as big as a Bigfoot, it was probably a bear that tourists simply magnified in their heads.

It was around that time that he had gone online and read stories from hikers who had been on the Marmot Trail, near the project area. Several of them had described the feeling of being watched from the fence that lined the trail, even being followed until the trail curved away from the enclosed forest. There had been claims of seeing shadowy figures in the trees, and even some growls when people wandered off-trail to get a closer look at the fence. The name Bigfoot Ridge had starting floating around online, and Cole had latched on to the term.

When they had arrived on Thursday, he had gone over to the project area and had rattled the gate. When that got no response, Laine had watched him use a spare branch to reach through the fence and try to knock it against a tree. The sound had been weak, but there was still a response in the form of something seeming to make its way through several large ferns, heading in a straight path to Cole. He had dropped the branch and backed away, and the movement had stopped. "There's something in there," he had breathed.

"Do you want to go in and see what it is?" Laine had asked. She was worried that the longer they stayed at the gate, the likelier it was that a ranger would come by and ask them to leave.

He shook his head. "No. Not right now." They left, and he had insisted on stopping at a hardware store to buy some paint and a small brush. That night, they had returned to the gate and he had painted the worlds "Bigfoot Ridge" above the official title on the sign. "Now I have someplace to talk about here," he said with triumph in his voice.

Earlier in the year, he had decided that Bobcat Lodge should have some sort of cryptid connected to it. "Bigfoot is not enough," he had insisted when Laine had argued that point. He had decided to pull out the fake costume he had built over the winter and pull a prank on the employees and visitors. Cole had found one of the viewing towers to be convenient for setting up a rope between several trees. The costume would fly along the rope, appear on a branch, and could be pulled back. Cole had started working on the imaginations of the resort guests during one of their long weekends back in May. The happiness on his face to hear people talking about a "flying Bigfoot thing" at breakfast one morning had made her realize how much he craved attention.

"I'm surprised Jenna or Donnie haven't found that costume yet. It was a big risk to stash it on the platform."

Cole shrugged as he put on his jacket. "It's in a metal box, and I'd bet Jenna and Donnie are way too busy with the guests in the lodge itself to be checking out everything on the trails. Come on. We're leaving tomorrow. This is our last chance to scare Nate and his friends."

Laine sighed and reached for her fleece coat. "Fine. But take it with you this time when we leave. I like this place, and you already have people talking about flying monsters."

Cole grinned, and Laine's heart beat faster. He could irritate her some of the time, but she still found his enthusiasm attractive. "Good. Quick, let's get going before they go to sleep."

They slipped out of their cabin. There were plenty of lights along the paths, so they could see clearly as they crossed the property, walking past the lodge and the other cabins on the other side of it. As they approached Cabin Ten, they cut through the grassy area next to Cabin Nine, entered the forest, and continued on along a familiar path that helped them stay nearly undetected. They reached the viewing tower and looked up. No one was up on the platform, trying to get a nighttime view of the lake and the moonlight.

Just as Cole started to climb up the ladder, they heard rustling in some tree branches. "What was that?" Laine asked nervously, her hair suddenly standing on end.

"The wind, probably," Cole whispered. "Come on. There's nothing here, remember?"

She waited until he reached the platform before starting up the ladder. Halfway up, she heard a growling noise from somewhere near the tree. Cole must have heard it, too, because he looked over the side. "Was that you?" he asked, a concerned expression on his face.

"No," she hissed. She looked around and gasped. Several trees away, she thought she saw something tall and dark standing near a tree trunk. *Not just tall*, she corrected herself. *Massive*. She hastened to get up to the platform, and was relieved to feel Cole's hands helping her up.

"Do you see that?" she asked, pointing to where she had seen the shape. It was no longer there. She looked around, but didn't see it.

"No. Come on, let's do this."

Cole lifted up the top of the box and picked up the costume he had created at home. It had the head and shoulders of an ape, with a button inside that intermittently activated the red, glowing eyes. The rest of it was just a dark, scruffy blanket, added to get the sense of an actual body shape, with an edge that looked like a wing.

He had noticed that, in the dark, once people saw what they considered to be a monster's eyes, the rest of the shape was pretty much meaningless. Some people ran away when the red glow appeared. One person earlier in the summer, walking on the lake trail, had used a flashlight to determine that whatever was in the tree was some stupid hoax. Cole had sat near that person the next morning and listened to him crowing about the fake creature and dismissing anyone who believed in "that monster crap." Cole knew that would happen on occasion. He had certainly heard enough stories during his interviews that made him question the honesty of the person telling him the tale.

He hooked up the monster head to the rope and retrieved the controller. At first, he had wanted to set up some sort of pulley system to control the monster, but the space between the trees made that almost impossible. It had been difficult enough to ask Jenna and Donnie for the use of a ladder without explaining what he was up to in the forest. They had barely believed his story about thinking he saw some fur high up on a tree limb. Instead, he had put a small motor in the monster that allowed him to remotely control the costume from the platform. It could travel in a straight line back and forth on the rope.

He was just about to set the costume free on the rope when the platform suddenly started shaking. Laine fell down, but grabbed on to a rail. He managed to stay standing, but the controller fell out of his hands and on to the platform. "What the hell?" he asked when the tree was still once again.

A growling sound from below them made his blood turn cold. Laine crawled across the platform and looked down through the hole to the ground. She screamed.

The massive creature she had seen earlier had returned. It was over nine feet tall and, she guessed, probably over seven hundred pounds. Its conical head and long arms pointed to it being Bigfoot. Its face was turned up at her, and she saw human-looking eyes in an ape-like face. It saw her and made a motion with its mouth, appearing to bare its teeth at her. Its hands were human-like, but huge, and she screamed again when the creature put its arms around the tree trunk and once again shook the tree.

This time, Cole lost his balance. The costume and the controller both slid off the rope and the platform and fell to the forest floor below. The creature saw the items and stepped back from the tree. It moved in the direction of the costume, and seemed to be curious about what it found. It picked up the ape head and shoulders and sniffed them.

"Laine, let's go." Cole suddenly didn't care if anyone found the costume. He wanted to get himself and Laine out of harm's way. He had never honestly expected to encounter

Bigfoot up close, and now that it was in front of them, he only wanted it to be gone. The smell that he had suddenly noticed was almost gagging him, and he had felt how easily the creature had shaken the tree. He didn't want to find out what it could do to him and Laine.

Laine was shaking. She coughed, also suddenly aware of the smell. The creature was still looking at the costume, turning its head back and forth, appearing to be confused. Its back was to them. She felt Cole's hands on her shoulders, urging her to go down the ladder, and she numbly nodded. Keeping an eye on the monster, she climbed down as quietly as she could.

Cole followed. In his haste, he missed the last two rungs of the ladder and landed hard on the ground. Bigfoot turned and saw them, and roared. Keeping the costume in hand, the creature started walking in their direction. Laine felt the ground shake from the creature's steps, and she struggled to get up. Cole, unhurt from his jump, grabbed her arm. "Run," he hissed. Laine followed him and they ran down the trail, screaming and shouting for help. The creature followed them, waving the costume around and roaring again. Its huge body allowed it to follow them at more of a walking pace, although it seemed to be right on their trail.

Finally, they broke free from the forest and found themselves on the lawn outside Cabin Ten. The creature stopped just inside the tree line. It roared again, and threw the costume in their direction. Then, it disappeared into the darkness. Cole fell to the ground, in shock at what he had just witnessed. Laine felt completely drained. She curled up and started crying, only stopping when she felt comforting hands on her shoulders.

"What was that?" Mike asked, sitting up. They had been lounging around the living room of the cabin, talking about their trip to Bigfoot Ridge the next day. Tiffany had an ice pack on her ankle, and Autumn and Nate had been sitting at the table. Autumn was updating her journal with notes about their logging road adventure, and Nate had been looking over the copies they had made at the library.

A scream came from the forest. "Anything on the camera?" Nate asked. Mike opened his laptop and shook his head. "Nope. Some tree limbs moving. That's about it."

Then, they heard a roar. "There's something out there," Tiffany said, removing her ice pack and standing up. She gently limped over to the kitchen window. "I don't see anything, though."

They heard shouts and screams, and cries for help. "Something's wrong," Autumn said, and opened the front door. Mike and Nate followed her around the porch.

The four of them were just in time to watch as Cole and Laine emerged from the forest, running away from something that was chasing them. Autumn stepped closer to see if she could get a glimpse of whatever creature was following them, but then looked up at the camera near her bedroom window. She hoped that would get a better view of the trail's end.

Nate gasped and pointed. A large creature stood at the edge of the forest. They couldn't see much except for its size. "Oh crap," Mike said. "That's what we're looking for."

The creature threw something from the forest and disappeared. Autumn heard tree limbs cracking and moving around and followed the creature's path with her eyes. She was tempted to simply run after it, but her attention was brought back to the situation by Laine's sobs.

She hurried over to Laine and wrapped her arms around her. "It's okay. It's over," she whispered soothingly. Laine stopped crying, but she was still shaking. Autumn sat down next to her and kept her arms around her. She knew she could provide little comfort after what Laine had just experienced, but she could at least try to let her know she wasn't alone.

Nate and Mike were tending to Cole. Tiffany went back into the cabin and got some blankets, and they managed to get Laine and Cole calm enough to stand up and walk. They guided them to the porch. Some people from nearby cabins had gathered on the lake path, but Autumn assured them that her friends had everything in hand. "Laine and Cole thought they saw something out in the forest," she explained. "You know how creepy the woods can be at night."

"Absolutely," one man said. "But what about the noises we heard? That must have been some big animal."

"Probably Bigfoot," someone else said, and that brought some laughter from the crowd.

"Yeah, right. You thought you saw Bigfoot the other day and it turned out to be your cousin in a long coat," someone joked. The crowd dispersed, everyone going back to their cabins.

Autumn saw two more people making their way down the path, one running and one strolling. Donnie reached them first, anxiously looking at Cole and Laine. "We heard those roars," he explained.

"And then we looked out and saw people gathering down this way," Jenna added as she walked up behind her husband. "Sorry, Donnie. You know I don't run."

He smiled briefly, then turned back to guests. "I'm going to take a look around the edge of the trail."

"I'll go with you," Nate offered. He picked up a flashlight and the two men headed around the side of the cabin. Tiffany emerged with some tea for Laine and Cole. They both gratefully took the cups and sipped. Laine closed her eyes, and opened them again abruptly.

"It was so quiet, at first," she said. "Who knows how long it was following us."

"Laine," Cole warned, but she shook her head.

"They're about to find out, anyway, Cole."

"Yes, I guess we are," Donnie interrupted. He and Nate came around to the front of the porch and Donnie held up the ape costume. "I'm guessing this is the supposed Batsquatch people have been talking about?"

Autumn's heart dropped as her thoughts moved from the monster they may have caught on camera. The focus was now on Cole and this hoax he had arranged. She could ask

Mike about the footage on his computer later.

"Okay, yes, I put that together to try to get some stories going about a cryptid here at the resort. I've been asking the people living over on the other side of the lake about what they may have seen and heard regarding the place known as Bigfoot Ridge. I thought if people were seeing something over on this side of the lake, the people in that neighborhood would open up to me." He shook his head sadly. "That group is pretty tight-lipped about monsters in the forest."

"Yes, Faye Carson told us about that," Nate said. "Maybe they just don't want to share anything publicly."

"More likely there's just nothing over there," Jenna stated impatiently.

Cole stared at her. "You sound just like one of the women I spoke to across the lake."

"Cole kept the costume in a box on that viewing tower closest to this cabin," Laine said, getting back to the moment. "We're leaving tomorrow, and this is my last planned trip here, so he decided that it would be perfect to show the cryptid hunters what they wanted to see."

"I've seen hoaxes before," Autumn said, with anger in her voice. "And I don't understand it. People will never believe you now if you claim you've actually seen what you were hoaxing."

"You saw what was chasing us, right?" Cole asked defensively. "We definitely weren't making that up."

"We saw it," Mike said. "That's probably the only reason we're still listening to you right now."

"I'm sorry about the fake Batsquatch," Cole said, looking directly at Jenna and Donnie. "I didn't activate it often, and never around kids."

"Well, that's good," Jenna said. "Even though kids heard the stories about it."

Cole shrugged. "That's unavoidable. You sell books about Bigfoot in your gift shop. There's talk about cryptids all over the state. I just made sure no kids were staying in this cabin before I let the costume fly out to the edge of the trees."

Jenna and Donnie looked at each other, then nodded. "I think you got your punishment for that tonight, with whatever was chasing you," Jenna said. "I won't say anything about the hoax as long as you take that costume with you when you leave. You're welcome to come back here anytime, both of you, without that thing. And believe me, we'll check to see if anything new shows up on the viewing towers."

"Thank you," Laine said. She glared at Cole. "We will be burning it when we get home."

He nodded in agreement. They finished their tea and stood. Laine motioned for Autumn to talk to her alone. Autumn followed her to the lake path and noticed there was still some wariness in Laine's eyes.

"You've seen one before, haven't you? A Bigfoot?" Laine asked bluntly.

"Yes. More than once."

"Did it get any easier to process the second time around?"

"Not really. It still just blows my mind that Bigfoot is alive and so varied in size and strength from creature to creature."

"Be careful if you go out to Bigfoot Ridge tomorrow. I got the sense, from Cole's attempted interviews, that people are protective of that land and whatever it holds."

"Thank you."

"Thank you for helping us." Laine hugged Autumn. She turned back to the porch. "Let's go, Cole. Time to try to get some sleep."

Cole waved to everyone, collected the costume from Donnie, and followed Laine down the path. Autumn returned to the porch. "Hopefully any talk of a Batsquatch will die down soon," Donnie said. "With no more sightings, the story should disappear."

"If we're lucky," Jenna agreed. "I'm tired. Let's get back to bed." She grabbed Donnie's hand and said goodnight to the group, then they followed Cole and Laine down the path to the lodge.

"So, Cole is a hoaxer. I wonder if his story about Bigfoot Ridge has any merit," Nate said once they had all retreated back into the cabin and locked the front door.

"Faye's story had some merit. Laine seemed to think there was something there," Autumn said. "And even though Ranger Tyler didn't give permission for us to go there, he seemed resigned to the fact that we were going to get inside the area."

"I think it's still worth exploring," Mike said. "But we need to be up early, so we should get to bed."

"Yes, I'm tired," Tiffany said as she finished rinsing out the mugs. "And my ankle hurts. Let's get started on this again in the morning."

They all said goodnight. Autumn walked up to her loft and shut the curtain, then changed into her pajamas. She sat up for another half an hour, writing about the found costume and the creature that had chased Laine and Cole out of the forest. She turned off her bedside light, ready to get some rest before exploring Bigfoot Ridge in the morning.

CHAPTER 14

When Autumn woke up, she went straight to the window and looked out. There was no sign that anything strange had happened last night. There were two deer grazing at the edge of the forest, a few squirrels running across the grass, and the sun was out. She looked overhead. A few clouds were in sight, but there was no rain in the forecast. After yesterday's rainfall, she was hoping that maybe they could find some good tracks today.

She heard someone moving around downstairs and hurried into the bathroom to clean up and get dressed. She kept her curtain shut as she removed her backpack from the top of the dresser and took everything out, re-packing it slowly to make sure she had everything she would need for the day. She placed her empty water bottle on the side; she'd fill it downstairs. She placed several plastic sample vials, a kit that included tweezers and a small pocketknife, and small plastic bags in the outer pocket. The inner pocket held an extra shirt and pair of socks, a map of the area, and a few small packages of trail mix in a small, bear-proof container.

Before leaving the house on Saturday, she had gone into the garage and looked through Zach's supplies. She had retrieved, and brought with her to the resort, a canister of bear spray. She secured it to the outside of her backpack. She didn't think they'd need any flashlights, but she placed a small one in her bag anyway. She decided to leave her journal here in the cabin, in case her bag got wet or stolen, as had happened on previous occasions. Satisfied with her personal preparations, she opened the curtain and started down the staircase.

Tiffany was already up and sitting on the couch, with her leg elevated on the coffee table. Nate handed her an ice pack and smiled at Autumn. "Morning. Get any sleep?"

"Yeah," she said. "It was surprisingly easy to fall asleep

after Laine and Cole went back to their cabin. I guess at some point during the night, the adrenaline just disappeared."

"Hopefully it will be back up today," Nate said. "Tiffany, are you sure you want to come with us? You could stay here."

She shook her head. "I don't mind staying in the car and keeping an eye out for approaching park rangers. You're not planning to be there all day, are you?"

"We'll be out of there before dark," Autumn assured her. "And if we're not seeing anything that could be leading to Bigfoot within a few hours, I'm guessing we probably won't be there for much longer than that." She filled her water bottle and secured it to her bag, on the opposite side from the bear spray. Nate saw the spray canister and caught her eye.

"I have some of that, too," he said. "Do you we should bring a taser?"

"I don't have one, and I think the spray should be enough to give us time to get away," Autumn said. For some reason, she felt squeamish at the idea of using a taser against a Bigfoot. Even though she had been in very close proximity to one before, and had seen how powerful and sometimes violent they could be, she still felt using caution and staying a certain distance from the creature should be enough to get them out of danger. If not, the spray would incapacitate the creature for a period of time, and it would eventually recover.

"I have a knife," Mike said from the doorway of his bedroom. His hair was combed back neatly, and he looked as well-rested as Autumn felt. "And there's a baseball bat in the car, if one of us wants to carry it."

Nate looked at him. "I don't think we'll need the bat."

"Do you not remember our dogman encounter last month?" Mike asked. "When it had someone pinned to the ground, and you tased it? You know how quickly monsters can attack."

"Different creatures," Nate argued. He paused, and Autumn saw a look of determination on his face. "Is there a taser with your equipment?"

"Yes," Mike said. He retreated into his bedroom and returned with the small weapon. "Why don't you carry it? That way each of us has a way to get away from anything that might attack us out there. Deer, bear, or Bigfoot, we'll be prepared."

Tiffany smiled. "Do you realize how freaking crazy you all sound?"

"Yes," they replied in unison.

"I'm packed and ready to get some breakfast," Autumn said. "You guys ready?"

"Yep." Mike pulled his backpack out of his room and plunked it down on the coffee table, keeping away from Tiffany's ankle. "Plaster and water for tracks. We're already covered with our defensive weapons. I have my laptop and an extra battery in here. I have speakers, so our call blasts can be heard at a longer distance. I have no idea what the terrain is, so we want to give Bigfoot a chance to hear the calls. We'll find some sticks and do some tree knocks. Do we have a time frame for all of this?"

"I told Tiffany that three hours or so should be sufficient to at least get a sign there's something there," Autumn said. "And we'll go from that point. If we see tracks, or if there's any responses to our calls, we'll stay out longer."

"As long as you're out of there before dark," Tiffany said firmly.

"You know, I was kind of hesitant about this before last night," Nate said. "Given how urgently Cole seemed to be directing us over to Bigfoot Ridge, I thought maybe he was planning some surprises for us. After their encounter, though, I don't think that'll be an issue."

"If anything, it sounds like Cole and Laine actually got whatever creature was chasing them pretty riled up," Autumn agreed. "Maybe that will work in our favor today."

They finished packing their gear and walked it all over to

Mike's SUV in the parking lot. They retreated to the lodge and settled down in the dining room for breakfast. When Autumn was wandering around the buffet, she looked across the dining room to see if Laine and Cole were present. Donnie, just coming out of the kitchen, caught her eye. "They left earlier this morning, if you were looking for Laine and Cole," he said. "I doubt we'll see them again until spring, but I'm sure they'll be back."

"I hope so. Despite Coal's dumb hoax idea, he's pretty good at getting people to share monster stories and make them public. And Laine seemed pretty smart."

"She is. I'm sure her hotel will be expanding to Port Mason in the next year or two." He noticed an empty tray and picked it up. "See you later."

Autumn returned to the table and reported that Laine and Cole were gone. "I don't think we need to worry about anything glowing through the trees tonight."

They finished breakfast and left the lodge. Mike got behind the wheel, Tiffany got comfortable in the passenger seat, and Nate and Autumn climbed into the backseat. He turned right out of the resort and drove down the highway. When they reached the turnoff with the sign for the ranger station, he slowed down and made the turn.

"Are we going to stop and check in with Ranger Tyler?" he asked. "He didn't exactly encourage us to come out here yesterday, but he seemed to know that we'd do it anyway."

"I think I'd feel better that someone knows we're in the area," Nate said. "Even if it means they'll try to stop us."

Autumn agreed. Her past experiences had taught her to try to be as safe as possible when heading out to the forest. "Let's go ahead and check in."

Mike turned into the ranger station parking lot. There was one official park vehicle in the lot, with a sedan and a truck sitting in the shade under a tree at the edge of the building. Nate and Autumn climbed out of the car and entered the station. A uniformed ranger sat at the front desk and smiled at them. His nameplate read "A. Washington."

"Hi, welcome to Olympic National Park," he said. "How can I help you?"

"Is Ranger Jake Tyler here?" Nate asked.

Ranger Washington shook his head. "No, sorry. He's out patrolling the area."

"We're staying at Bobcat Lodge, and we heard there were some trails over on this side of the lake that we could check out," Autumn said. "Is there anything interesting to see over this way?"

"Of course," Ranger Washington grinned. "Here, this is a map of Bobcat Lake." He highlighted a trail and turned the single piece of paper around to show them. "This is the ranger station here. Turn left out of this lot and keep going down this road. The road curves, but just before the curve you'll see a pretty popular area for hiking, the Marmot Trail. I've already directed a few people there this morning."

"Anything else along this road?" Autumn asked.

"A little further down, there's a closed-down research area where we let scientists examine the natural rock and plants without the interference of hikers," Ranger Washington explained. "There's a fence around the area, so you'll know if you go too far. The public is not allowed inside the gate."

"Thanks," Nate said. "Would you let Ranger Tyler know that Autumn Hunter and her friends stopped by? We met him yesterday."

"Sure will." The ranger made a note on a piece of paper. "Good luck out there. Hope you can get some great pictures. It's good weather today."

"Thank you," Autumn said. She and Nate left the building and got back into the SUV. Nate showed everyone the map.

"He's trying to get us to take this trail, which is about half a mile down the road from the entrance to Bigfoot Ridge. He described the ridge as a fenced-off research area, so that's what we're looking for. That's good. That means privacy for us."

"The fence doesn't work if the Bigfoot we saw last night is the same creature that's roaming around over here," Mike said. "And the chances of that are pretty good."

They drove out of the ranger station lot just as another car turned in, and headed left as Ranger Washington had suggested. Autumn turned around and noticed a park service truck turning in to the ranger station lot, and she assumed it was Ranger Tyler, returning to the office. She was honestly hoping that at some point he might come looking for them, because the idea of being in an enclosed area with a Bigfoot was sending chills down her spine. All her previous encounters had been in open areas with escape options. This would present more of a challenge.

They slowed down around the bend in the road and saw the Marmot Trail. Four cars were in the lot, and a couple of people were just setting out along the trail. Signs explained the rules of the park, and there was even a portable toilet. This was obviously the trail where guests were expected to stay on the path and not wander off into the woods. Autumn wondered how close to the trail the fence for Bigfoot Ridge extended.

"Here we are," Mike announced. They pulled up in front of a large, solid metal gate. The familiar "No Trespassing" signs were posted on either side. Mike was able to pull the SUV up along the side of a six-foot-tall chain link fence.

"Bobcat Lake Research Project. You must have a permit to enter this area and be accompanied by a ranger," Nate read from the sign on the gate when they had all gotten out of the car. "All trespassers will be removed by park law enforcement and subject to fines. No camping. No overnight stays."

"That doesn't sound suspicious at all," Autumn said with a sarcastic smile. "Even the scientists had to have a ranger here at all times. Faye mentioned they had set up cameras, so there was no reason for them to stay here overnight."

"Bigfoot Ridge," Mike said, getting a couple of pictures of the painted-on phrase.

Tiffany rattled the fence. "This couldn't keep in anything the size of the creature we saw last night. It wouldn't keep it out, either, if it wanted to get in."

"Should we leave the car parked along the fence here?" Mike asked. "The tree limbs should provide shade for Tiffany all day, and it's not likely that many people will pass by this place. There are those cabins further down the road, but I think most visitors will probably stop at the Marmot Trail."

"I'm okay with that," Tiffany said. "I'll handle anyone who comes by."

"Let's get going then," Nate said. "Let's see if this place really lives up to the name of Bigfoot Ridge."

Autumn joined Mike and Nate in getting their gear from the back of the car. They closed the back door, and Mike handed the keys to Tiffany. Nate made sure she had everything she needed, placing the cooler on the driver's seat so she could reach it. She left the window halfway and waved at them as they reached the metal gate.

It was as tall as the chain link fence, but Mike quickly discovered that they could use the fence as a foothold to get over the gate. He led the way, pausing at the top. "I don't see anyone here," he said. "Good." He scrambled down and stood in full sight of Nate and Autumn. "Hurry, before someone comes along."

Autumn was next. She placed her foot into one of the holes in the fence and used the gate to steady herself. She climbed to the next hole, and was able to look over the front area of the property. There were faint tracks on a road wide enough for vehicles, and the tracks led off into the distance. There was a sign-in station near the gate, as well as the same type of portable toilet they had seen at the hiking trail, and also a hand-washing station. Autumn let Mike help guide her down the other side, and when she landed, she immediately went over to the sign-in station to look at the book inside of it.

Nate got over the fence and landed next to Mike. "Okay, we're here," he said. "Where do we start?"

"I say we follow these tire tracks," Mike said. "Someone's been here recently."

"Friday," Autumn called out. She placed the book back into a wood box and closed it. "I guess old habits die hard. Ranger Tyler actually signed in and out. He was here for ten minutes."

"We're on our own," Nate said. Something about the words made Autumn's hair stand on end, and she willed herself to not be nervous. This was just like all the other Bigfoot investigations they had conducted over the years. Even without the rest of their team she was certain they could find some evidence of the creature.

"Let's go," she said firmly, and started down the road. Nate and Mike followed her. She kept her eyes on the horizon, not willing to admit to either of her friends that she already felt that they were being watched.

CHAPTER 15

They had walked for thirty minutes when Autumn stopped. She pointed down at the edge of the road. "Is that a footprint in the mud?" she asked. She stepped closer, careful to avoid stepping in the track itself.

Mike got out his camera and took several pictures. "Looks like one. The mud's still fresh here, under the tree cover."

Nate retrieved a tape measure from his bag and laid it down next to the track. "Eighteen inches by seven inches," he said. Autumn noted that in her phone. "And it looks like there are two more heading off in that direction."

"Should we get a cast?" Mike asked. They had only attempted to get a cast of a footprint once before, and had failed to keep it in one piece. It had crumbled and become useless to them.

"No harm in trying," Autumn said. Mike set his bag down and pulled out the plaster mix and water. Following directions, he mixed the wet plaster in a small bowl and gently poured the mix into the track.

"It should sit for at least thirty minutes, preferably an hour," Mike said. "Do you think those other tracks are worth casting?"

Nate shook his head. "Partials. This is the best and deepest track."

Autumn looked around them. The sun shone through the trees in some places, and there were some clear-cut areas in the forest. The tracks they were looking at now led through one of those areas. She could see something large in the distance. From here it appeared to be some sort of structure, perhaps a shelter set up by the researchers for observation. She was interested in seeing it, however, so she pointed to it.

"Let's go take a look over there," she said. "I'm curious about those tree limbs that are sticking up through the other trees and plants."

They picked up their gear and walked through the forest. As they walked, Autumn became aware that the deeper they went into the woods, the fewer sounds they were hearing. Nate noticed it, too. "It's quiet," he said, his tone ominous. "I think we might be getting close to something."

Mike looked around. His camera was still in his hand. He took a few pictures of something off in the distance. "Not sure what that was," he mumbled.

When they reached the structure, Autumn circled around it once in amazement. Tree limbs had been piled against each other to create a rough-looking structure. Fern leaves and other smaller bushes and branches had been used to fill on the gaps, creating a layer that made it difficult to see into the shelter from anyplace other than the entrance, which was roughly six feet tall. Whatever lived in here would have to duck down to get into the structure.

They had seen a similar structure back in Tahoma Valley. The people they had spoken to about that structure believed it had been built by Bigfoot, and they had taken it down. Autumn took out her phone to get some pictures of her own while Mike and Nate got close to the structure.

"These limbs were torn down," Nate said, touching the ends of some of the heavy branches. "See how uneven these edges are?"

"It's got to be, what, ten feet tall?" Autumn asked.

"Closer to twelve," Mike said.

She joined them at the tall oblong hole that seemed to be the entrance and winced. The smell of decomposition and animal feces was overwhelming. Nate shined his flashlight inside and the beam stopped on several bones sitting in a pile at the edge of the shelter.

"I hope those are animal bones," Mike said. He frowned at his camera screen. "I can't get a good angle from here."

"I'll do it," Autumn offered. Mike handed her the camera and Autumn took a deep breath before stepping inside the shelter.

The smell made her eyes water, but she got close to the pile of bones. She looked at them closely and thought she saw what could be a deer skull. There was no sign of any human victims, and that brought a small sense of relief. She took several photos of the bones. What she saw when she turned around sent chills down her spine.

Several items of human clothing were piled together. She took some pictures with Mike's phone, then pulled out her own for backup evidence. "What is that?" Nate asked. "Clothes?"

She nodded. "I think Bigfoot has made a bed out of them." She bent down. "Hey, can one of you get a couple of vials out of my backpack?"

"I'm coming inside," Nate said, and she felt him unzip her bag. "You want this little leather bag here, too?"

"Yes. Thanks." She took it from him and used the tweezers to get a couple of hair samples. They were long and coarse, and dark. "Should we take one of these shirts?" she asked. The clothing did not look torn or bloody. It simply looked like the creature had collected items left behind by campers or backpackers and placed them in a long, wide pile on the dirt floor.

"No, I think the pictures are enough."

"Um, Autumn? Nate? I feel like we should be moving on," Mike said. "And I'd also like my camera back."

"No problem," Autumn said. "I need fresh air."

They backed out of the shelter. Autumn walked around the clearing again and saw a few spots of blood on a bush. "Over here," she said, and got out another vial. "That rotting flesh smell is stronger here," she said, and started looking through the plants.

A short search turned up the body of a raccoon. There were clear bite marks around what remained of its abdomen and legs. "Bigfoot bites," Nate murmured as he took photos.

This time, Autumn got out her knife and leaned over the raccoon. She gently cut out a small piece of bitten flesh and placed it in one of the vials. She placed her kit back in her bag. There were no other dead animals in the immediate area of the structure, and no signs that people other than themselves had been here recently. The bed inside the structure was an oddly human feature of the shelter, and Autumn though that this Bigfoot simply wanted to be left alone to live its life.

She handed Mike his camera. "Did you see something?" Nate asked.

"I heard a couple of growls from that direction," Mike said, pointing further back in the forest. "Maybe we should back to the road and find a place to set up for some call blasts."

"Sure," Nate said. Autumn took one last look around the structure, then followed her friends through the forest and back to the road. They followed it for about twenty more minutes, before it ended in a wide clearing.

Several tables had been set up under a makeshift tent shelter at the far end of the clearing. When they reached the tent, Autumn looked to her right and pointed to the view. "Look. You can see the ocean in the distance."

"This must have been a great place for the researchers to sit when they were done for the day," Nate said. He placed his laptop on a table and looked around. "Faye mentioned how quickly they got out of here. They left behind some notebooks."

He opened his laptop. "Should we check those out while we're here?"

Autumn nodded. She retrieved a binder and opened it. "This must have been put together by the geologists. There are photos of the cliff and the large rocks over there. The fence ends where the rocks begin, so Faye was right that animals would be able to get in and out if they were nimble enough to maneuver over the terrain."

"You think that the Bigfoot could do it?" Nate asked.

Autumn took another look at the photos. "I'd be more willing to think that it probably tore apart a section of fence." She flipped through the rest of the book and didn't find anything else that interested her.

The biology notebook was more intriguing, as she flipped through the reports of how many types of animals were in the project area at the start. Coyotes, bobcats, cougars, various other mammals, and a few species of birds were all documented. They had even gotten a couple of pictures of a bear. In one of the photos, Autumn couldn't tell if the animal was a bear, or something else, and she understood how people could mistake it for a Bigfoot in certain conditions.

"I wonder how they explained that they wouldn't come back because of one bear," Mike said, helping Nate plug in his speakers. "Especially since there was already a bear here when they started the project."

"They probably explained that it was aggressive," Autumn said, closing the notebook. The data had abruptly stopped, and there had been no mention of the creature they had encountered on the last day.

Mike set up the speakers so that they were pointed east, in the direction away from the Marmot Trail. Someone over there might still hear it, but it would hopefully sound faint to any hikers over there. "I wonder how long the Bigfoot was here before they saw it?"

Autumn pondered that while she took a drink from her water bottle. She had often thought that people were having increased sightings of creatures like Bigfoot because all forest animals were losing some of their natural territory. That didn't seem to apply here, but maybe the creature had heard the humans and escaped during the times that they were active in the project area. She opened the notes folder on her phone and updated it for their morning activities, then sat back on a bench while Nate brought up the vocal samples for call blasting.

The first call that came through always chilled her. It was a famous one that had been used in Bigfoot investigations for many years. No scientific examination had ever identified the animal that had made the call, and it was strongly believed to be the call of a Bigfoot.

Nate played the call once, and they waited for five tense minutes, hoping for a response. "Nothing?" Nate asked.

"Nothing," Mike confirmed.

"Let's try this one," Nate said. The second one was a call that they had recorded on their first group investigation after meeting through the BOG forums. He played it twice, letting the noise die down before picking up his own bottle of water to drink.

This time, they got a response. Autumn set down the vials, which she had been marking with the date and location of retrieval. A howl sounded through the trees. It was distant, but it was definitely a response from an animal. "Was that a wolf?" Mike whispered.

"There are no wolves in Olympic National Park," Autumn said. "At least, no natural ones."

"You don't really think there's a dogman here, do you?" Nate asked. His close encounter with the creature had unnerved him.

"I don't know, but remember the claw marks we've seen twice now, on the door and the deer," Autumn said. "I guess it could be a coyote making that noise, but it sounded like it came from a larger animal."

"Let's try this third call," Nate said. This was a call they had found online at the suggestion of other cryptid groups. The sound was long and mournful, sounding very much like something was sad or in pain. He played the call twice.

This time, the response was instant. There was a loud roar

and tree limbs started shaking at the other end of the clearing. "I think we have company," Mike whispered.

Autumn, painfully reminded of past evidence she had lost, made sure the vials went back in her backpack. "Let's see what happens," she said. She eyed the entrance to the clearing. Movement in the bushes indicated that a large animal was several feet away from their only exit.

Autumn pulled out her phone and started a video. Nate played the first call again. This also got a response, but it sounded like the creature had retreated deeper into the forest. There were shaking plants beyond the tree line. "Are you getting this?" Nate asked quietly.

"Yes," she whispered back. She stood and started walking slowly in the direction of the shaking limbs.

"Autumn," Mike hissed. "Come back."

She shook her head and kept walking. "Play it again," she called. Nate did, and this time the result was more than she could have hoped for.

A giant, hairy creature stepped out from behind a tree. It was over nine feet tall, with dark hair. Its eyes, even from this distance, looked human, while its face was that of an ape. It was muscular, with long arms and a conical head. Autumn held her ground as she filmed the animal, aware that her hands had started shaking.

It pounded the tree, and the tree moved. Autumn felt fear making her heart beat faster. She imagined what this creature could do to all of them if it felt disturbed enough to defend its territory. The creature took a step in her direction, and she backed away. It balled its hands into fists, opened its mouth, and roared. She dropped her phone and bent to pick it up again. When she looked up, the creature had disappeared back into the forest.

"Come on, Autumn," Mike whispered. He had snuck up behind her and gently grabbed her arm. She tensed up, then relaxed.

"Did you get pictures?" she asked. She kept an eye on the trees as Mike guided her back to the tent.

"Yes," he said. She saw that Nate had shut down his computer and placed it back into his bag. He unplugged the speakers with trembling hands.

"No need for tree knocks," he said. "I think we've successfully drawn it out."

"Let's check on the footprint cast and get out of here," Mike said. "I think we've got some good evidence. Enough to share with the forum and for you to include in your book, Autumn."

She was about to respond when Nate gasped. The creature had reappeared next to the tree. "Let's go," he said. "Hopefully it will let us leave."

"I think it knows we were in its home," Autumn said. "Look at how its sniffing in the air."

Indeed, the Bigfoot had its nose in the air, its head moving in jerky movements. Its eyes landed on the group again, and it growled. The sound, the same one that Mike had heard earlier, was loud and deep. Autumn suddenly realized that the creature might not let them leave peacefully.

As if reading her mind, the creature picked up a large rock, and hurled it at them. "How are we going to get out of here?" Mike hissed.

"There's only one way back to the gate," Autumn agreed. "Unless we split up."

Another roar brought a grim look to Nate's face. "Run for the road," he ordered. They left the tent. Bigfoot, seeing where they were heading, ran along the trees and stood at the entrance to the clearing.

"I guess we only have one other choice. We'll have to go through the woods," Autumn said. She started running in the direction of the trees where the creature had been standing when they had noticed it. Although the Bigfoot was fast, it couldn't make it back to her in time to keep her from entering the forest.

Autumn kept running once she got into the trees. Thankfully, the forest was fairly open here and the plants were grouped together in plots. She realized as she was running that this was probably where the botanists had conducted their plant studies.

She heard footsteps behind her and tripped over a fern. Uttering a short scream, she rolled a couple of times and came to a stop. She sat up and realized that it was Nate and Mike following her. "I thought you might have gone the other way," she teased them, out of breath. "As a distraction."

"We're not leaving you," Mike said. A roar came from behind them and Nate pulled Autumn up from the ground. "Come on, let's go." A rock landed near them, one large enough to crack their heads open. They turned and saw the creature approaching them, pausing only long enough to re-arm itself with another rock.

They passed several landmarks that were starting to look familiar. "I think I know where we are," Autumn said. She looked ahead and confirmed her thoughts. They were approaching the tree structure, the creature's home. She stumbled into the clearing and suddenly felt a searing pain run through her arm. She fell down again and rolled over. The Bigfoot entered the clearing before Mike and Nate and headed straight in her direction.

CHAPTER 16

"You're just giving me this message now?" Jake snapped at Aaron, looking down at the note the other ranger had handed to him. He had arrived back at the station over an hour ago and had been working on reports in his office when Aaron had come in and mentioned Autumn Hunter and her friends.

Aaron shrugged. "No one said it was urgent. I directed that woman and her friends to the Marmot Trail."

"I'd bet anything that they went to the Bobcat Lake Project instead," Jake said. He opened up a window on his computer and entered the password for the trail camera inside the gate. Sure enough, he recognized the three people who had climbed over the fence over an hour ago and were walking down the road. He stood and put on his jacket. He checked his gun to make sure it was loaded. "I met Autumn and her friends on the old logging road yesterday down by the resort. They told me they were here to look for Bigfoot."

"You think they went to Bigfoot Ridge?" Aaron asked, his eyes wide. While it was not a popular title among the rangers, they had all come around to accepting that monster hunters had recently started referring to the area by that name.

"Yes." Jake hurried through the station. "I'll call if I need backup. Stay here for any visitors that may need your help."

"Be safe, Jake," Aaron called as Jake sailed through the door. Jake ran to his park service truck and got in. As he started the engine, he considered calling for another law enforcement ranger. He had never encountered a creature such as Bigfoot in person, but he reasoned that they were still just animals and could be injured. He had his gun and his taser, and he prayed that the group had also brought their own weapons to use if they needed to defend themselves.

He left the parking lot and drove down the road, staying just above the speed limit. He drove around the curve and noticed that the Marmot Trail was popular today. He thought he recognized two people that were just getting out of their car. John and Beth Britten appeared to be making another attempt at the Marmot Trail today.

Several other people were milling around the parking lot, chatting by their cars. He focused his eyes ahead and drove until he saw a familiar SUV parked alongside the fence that surrounded the research area.

He made a turn in the road and pulled up behind the SUV. He could see that someone had been left behind in the car, and as he approached the vehicle, he recognized the light blonde hair of the woman who had been limping yesterday. "Hi," he called out as he approached the open window. "Park ranger."

The woman was sitting tensely, her hands on her phone. "Oh, Ranger Tyler. Thank God," she said. "I've been hearing some disturbing sounds coming from the forest for the past several minutes, and my phone isn't working right here. I was thinking about driving to the ranger station but I didn't want to abandon my friends."

"Tiffany, right?" he asked, recalling the names from yesterday. "And Autumn, Nate, and Mike are in Bigfoot Ridge."

"Yes," she said. "I don't know what they were doing for the past hour, but I could hear it when they played some call blasts. Those are..."

"I'm familiar with the term," Jake said.

"Then I heard some roars. After that, I started getting nervous. I don't know what's going on in there."

"Can you drive?"

"Yes. It was my left leg that was injured yesterday."

"I want you to take this vehicle back to the ranger station," he ordered. "You can stay in the parking lot there. If Ranger Washington comes out to speak to you, let him know that I told you to go there."

"Yes, sir." Tiffany opened the door, and he guided her around to the driver's seat. She moved the cooler and started the SUV. "They did bring some bear spray, like you suggested. They also have a knife, and I think they brought a taser with them." She was relieved now that someone had come to help. Horrifying pictures were running through her head, and she desperately hoped her friends were all right.

"Good. I hope they don't need to use any of it."

Tiffany drove away slowly, scanning the fence line as she went, seemingly looking for any sign of her friends. Jake returned to his truck and drove to the gate. He got out, unlocked the gate, then drove through. When he got back out of the truck, he closed the gate but didn't lock it. He knew the truck could drive through it without any major damage.

He returned to his truck and continued down the road, windows down, listening for any sounds of a chase or a fight. A roar sounded through the woods, and he almost drove into a tree. He had heard that sound before, in the woods around his father's cabin. Tate had claimed that it was a bear defending itself against another bear.

"Not a bear, Dad," Jake muttered, a brief flash of grief in his heart. He looked ahead and saw a puddle of white at the side of the road. Curious, he stopped and got out of the car.

He touched it and realized it was a plaster mold. He carefully lifted the edge and turned it over. His breath caught. It was a footprint. A large footprint. He had seen casts like these in museums, but never a freshly made one. Some instinct told him to preserve it, so he picked it up, wrapped it in a towel from his truck, and placed it on the back seat.

He set out into the forest, in the direction that whatever made those footprints had been headed. He could see a curious-looking tree formation in the distance. As he got closer, he noticed that the sounds around him had disappeared. It made him uneasy.

He heard shouts coming from somewhere in the forest. Near the tree structure up ahead, he saw four running figures. He recognized three of them as humans. Autumn and her friends had apparently caught the attention of the large creature following them. For a moment, his training made him think there was some sort of giant man on their trail. His eyes, though, immediately told him he was wrong.

The fourth figure made him pause, and he stood still, letting the scene in front of him process through his brain. The height was too tall, and the width and musculature were too large and powerful for a human. It had dark hair and its body resembled an ape, with long arms and massive hands. Those hands that were throwing a rock in the direction of one of the humans. He heard a scream and more shouts.

"Hey!" he called. He started running. He could see the creature standing still, looking down at the ground, and realized that someone had fallen. The creature bent down and picked up a heavy tree limb, raising it over his head. He stopped and pulled out his gun. Making sure no humans were in his view, he shot at the creature.

Autumn looked up at Bigfoot. She saw that a rock had hit her arm, and another wave of pain coursed through her. Mike and Nate had dropped down and were huddled together near a tree. She saw that Nate was digging through his backpack, looking for the taser. Mike, looking helpless, kept his camera up and was taking pictures of the creature. He finally dropped the camera and reached out to grab Autumn's backpack, which had fallen off her shoulders just before she reached the clearing.

The creature looked at Autumn with anger in its eyes. It bent down and pulled a tree limb from the base of the structure. She could see Nate sneaking up behind the creature, the taser in his hands, but she knew he'd be too late to help her. Autumn started crying as she realized what was about to happen, and wished she could see Zach again. It raised the tree limb over its head and glared at her, ready to bring it down on her head.

A shot rang out. The tree limb fell from the creature's hands and it roared in pain, grasping one hand in the other. The creature spun around, and hit Nate in the chest with its long arm. He yelled in surprise, dropped the taser, and stumbled over to a tree. He fell down, looking stunned and gasping for air.

Nate had given Mike some time to sneak up on Bigfoot's other side, and he was ready with the bear spray. The creature sensed him and flung his arm out again, but Mike ducked. He stepped closer and directed the spray at Bigfoot's face.

The creature roared again and backed away from all of them, waving its hand in the air and splattering blood across the ground. It blindly moved around the front of the shelter until it found the entrance and crawled inside. Moaning noises came from inside the structure, keeping them all aware that the Bigfoot was still alive.

"Hey!" a voice called. Autumn propped herself up with her right arm and saw Ranger Tyler approaching, his gun held down at his side. "Are you all okay?"

"Yes," Autumn said, her tears starting to subside. She felt the presence of Bigfoot, just a few feet away inside the structure. She turned and saw one of the creature's eyes watching her. A growl came from within the structure, and Mike placed the bear spray back on the side of Autumn's bag.

"I think we should get out of here," he said.

"That's a good idea," Ranger Tyler said. "Why don't you three head back to my truck, and I'll make sure this thing doesn't follow us."

"Are you going to kill it?" Autumn asked as Mike helped Nate to his feet. She grabbed her bag, putting it on her back as she also picked up Nate's bag. Another growl was heard from the shelter, and a face appeared at the entrance. Ranger Tyler moved around and pointed his gun at the creature. It backed out of sight, going deeper into the structure.

"Depends on what it does next," Ranger Tyler answered honestly. "Now, go."

Nate kept his arms against his side as they all walked back to the truck. On the way, Autumn gasped. "Blood!" she cried out. "We could get a sample."

"No," both men replied.

"You have the hairs and the animal skin," Mike added.

They got to the side of the road and noticed their plaster cast was missing. They opened the truck doors and Autumn pointed to the towel.

"Ranger Tyler picked it up," she said. Nate helped her up into the truck and looked at his phone, hoping to see that he could connect with Tiffany. There was still no signal.

"Are you okay?" Mike asked. "That was a strong hit."

"Just got the wind knocked out of me," Nate said. He took a few deep breaths and coughed. The initial pain in his chest was subsiding. "I think I'll be okay."

Autumn unwrapped the cast. It was a perfect track. She folded the towel back around it and placed it next to her on the seat. They had all gotten into the truck when they heard another roar. Five minutes later, Ranger Tyler appeared. He jogged through the forest and hurriedly got into the truck.

"Is it still alive?" Autumn asked.

"Yes," he said tensely. "Do you have any idea how crazy all of you are?"

"Yes," they responded in unison. Ranger Tyler shook his head and started laughing. His laugh was cut short as he looked up and saw the Bigfoot standing several feet off the road, watching them, blood still dripping from its hand.

"Go!" Autumn shouted, and Ranger Tyler obeyed. He gunned the truck down the road, kicking up dirt that sprayed over the Bigfoot. The creature roared and started to follow them. Ranger Tyler looked in his rearview mirror and swore, then increased his speed. He drove through the gate, braked hard, and got out.

"What are you doing?" Mike shouted.

"Locking the gate," Ranger Tyler said calmly. The Bigfoot was drawing close. Jake didn't know how a creature that large could move so quickly.

Autumn saw her chance. She grabbed the bear spray from her bag, gripping the can tightly with her right arm, and slid out of the car. She ran over and reached the gate just before Ranger Tyler shut it. The creature was there, its smell and heavy breathing overcoming her senses. It pushed against the gate hard enough to get its good hand through and grabbed Autumn's right arm, pressing on her wounds from the previous day.

She screamed and tried to step away, but the creature's grip was too strong. Ranger Tyler started to pull out his gun again, but she shook her head. She had one defense that she could use. She transferred the spray can to her injured arm and brought it up to Bigfoot's face She looked it right in the eyes and sprayed the creature again.

The creature stepped back and lost its balance. When it hit the ground, the gate shook and Ranger Tyler lost grip of the lock. He got it under control again and twisted the key. A growl from the other side of the gate let them know that the Bigfoot was still alive.

"Come on," Ranger Tyler said tersely. Autumn followed him to the truck and climbed back inside. They sat for a moment in silence, watching the gate. Just as they were about to pull away, Autumn saw the creature standing at the fence, looking at them while trying to wipe its face with its hand, leaving bloody trails across its face and chest.

"How does that thing get out? We thought maybe there was a hole in the fence," she said, her voice shaking, as Ranger Tyler pulled onto the road.

He shrugged. "The intent of the fence was to keep out people, not anything of that size and strength. Maybe that creature will stay away from humans whenever it can in the future."

"You've never seen it before while you were in there with the scientists?" Nate asked skeptically.

"No. The day that the scientists left, they claimed that there was a bear in there. From its behavior, it seemed like it was aggressive. One of my neighbors later told me that they had really seen a Bigfoot. Since I've always been skeptical regarding such creatures, I kept that information to myself."

"I wonder where Bigfoot went when the scientists were here," Nate said. "Maybe it stayed in the forest over around the lake, especially after the fire."

Ranger Tyler stiffened. "There was something at the lake before the fire. Something that left claw marks behind when my dad died there."

Autumn had managed to calm herself, but she felt compelled to bring up the idea of another creature. "Perhaps he was killed by a dogman."

Ranger Tyler swerved and quickly got control of the truck again. "Dogman? What the hell is that?"

"Those howls we've been hearing recently? There are no wolves around here. The scientists mentioned coyotes in their notes, but the creatures left the research area."

"Dogman," Ranger Tyler repeated the word, then fell silent.

He remembered John and Beth's story on Saturday. They had described a large wolf walking on its hand legs. It had apparently been following the wounded cougar. Would a dogman look like an upright wolf? He saw the crowds at the Marmot Trail and came back to the present, trying to clear the image from his head. He'd have to look into the possibility of another monster later.

Autumn thought about the danger she had faced for the rest of the ride. When they returned to the ranger station, they were relieved to see Tiffany. She had gone inside the station and was sitting near one of the displays, reading through some brochures and looking anxiously at her phone. Autumn saw that they had a signal here, so she walked away from the others and placed a call to Zach.

She smiled when she got his voice mail. Her voice teared up when she heard his voice. "Hi, Zach. We've had an exciting day, and well, I'm just glad that I'm able to leave you this message. Please call when you can. I love you." She hung up, wiped her eyes, and winced at the pain in her arm.

"What about the Bigfoot track?" Mike asked. "It's still in your truck."

Ranger Tyler shook his head. "I'm keeping that. It was taken on park service land."

Mike started to argue, but Autumn put her hand on his

arm. "It's okay," she said. "I think they have the ability to better preserve the track than we do." She turned to Ranger Tyler, wincing with pain again. "Will you let us know what you do with it?"

He nodded. "Can I see your wound?" Ranger Tyler asked. She let him look closely at her arm. She moved it around for him and flexed her elbow a few times. The pain was starting to subside. He suggested that she go to a clinic and get it looked at, and she didn't refuse. He also advised Nate to get his chest examined.

"Shall we get out of here?" Nate asked. He put an arm around Tiffany. "I know I'm ready to get back to our regular lives."

"Can we ever really do that after an encounter like this?" Autumn asked. She looked at the three-dimensional display of Bobcat Lake and the surrounding land that sat against the wall. The area where they had just been was marked in red as being off-limits for visitors. She wondered how many other Bigfoot hunters would ignore the warnings and go in anyway.

"We can try," Mike said softly. "Come on. Let's get Autumn to that clinic."

"Thank you, Ranger Tyler," Autumn said as the ranger followed them out to their car.

"Please, call me Jake."

"Jake, then. We really appreciate you coming to help us."

"Most people out here probably don't have an encounter like yours," Jake said. "And I think that's a good thing."

"Do you still think that Bigfoot that killed your dad?" Autumn asked.

"I don't know," he said, and shook his head. "I'd hate to think there's more than one monster out there."

Autumn wondered if she should have voiced her concern about a possible dogman. She had nothing to base her theory on except for claw marks and some howls that were most likely from a canine creature. "We'll be leaving tomorrow. I hope you don't have to go rescue any other Bigfoot hunters after we leave."

"We always have to keep an eye out for people wandering away from the trails," he said with a wink, and laughed. He waited until they were all in the car, then went back into the office.

After Autumn and her friends left, Aaron joined Jake. It was only early afternoon, but Jake was considering heading home for the day. Since he had fired his gun, though, he knew he'd have to contact his boss and fill out some paperwork. "Did they actually see Bigfoot?" Aaron asked, his voice nervous.

"It was an encounter none of us will ever forget. There's a reason it's called Bigfoot Ridge," Jake responded vaguely. They heard the front door open. "You better go greet those visitors."

Aaron walked out into the front room. "Jake!" he called out almost immediately. Jake reluctantly stood and walked back out to greet the new visitors. He was not surprised to see John and Beth standing with Aaron.

"Hi, Ranger Tyler," John said. "We finally made it all the way up the Marmot Trail."

"I'm glad to hear that," Jake said honestly. "Did you like the view?"

"Oh, yes," Beth said. "A lot of people kept saying they heard animal calls, and we thought we heard some, too. Anyway, we just wanted you to know that we saw that wolf thing again. It was climbing up the rocks on the cliff, and then it disappeared behind that fence. We got some pictures."

"Behind the fence," Jake repeated.

"Climbed the rocks," Aaron echoed.

John smiled. "Yes. Have a good day." He and Beth left the building with an air of triumph.

Aaron started to speak, but Jake shook his head. He had a lot to process in his head. He returned to his office and sat back in his chair. His mind reverted to the tree shelter, after Autumn and her friends had left to return to the truck.

He had almost put a couple more bullets into the creature

when it had started to come out of the shelter, but once it had seen his gun again, the creature had retreated. The feeling of being shot seemed to keep the creature at bay while Jake was able to make his own escape, although the effects had been short-lived since it had then pursued them to the gate. The creature's eyes had seemed eerily human despite the outward appearance of its body. He had felt killing it would be wrong and had given it a chance to survive. He also had a feeling this would not be his last encounter with Bigfoot.

CHAPTER 17

It was early evening when the group finally returned to the lodge. The nurse at the clinic had taken some x-rays and confirmed a light hairline fracture in Autumn's arm. She had been given a sling and some ice along with care instructions and was told to follow up with her doctor at home. Nate had some bruises, but the doctor that had examined his x-rays had confirmed that there were no internal injuries.

When she had questioned the cause of their injuries, they had explained that they had been hiking and tried to do some off-trail exploring. Mike had assured both the doctor and the nurse that they had reported the incident to the park rangers. On the way back to the lodge, Nate offered to drive Autumn home the next day. They had driven Tiffany's car to the resort, so it made sense for Tiffany to drive on her own and pick him up at Autumn's house.

They entered the lodge, having agreed to eat before going back to their cabin to review all the footage. Jenna was at the reception desk and her jaw dropped when she saw Autumn. "What happened?" she asked, her face filled with concern. "Were you injured hiking?"

"I guess you could say that," Autumn said. She leaned closer and whispered. "I was attacked by Bigfoot."

Jenna stepped back and rolled her eyes. "Like I'm going to believe that." She shook her head. "Whatever happened, I'm glad you're okay. At least it wasn't the Batsquatch." She winked.

Autumn burst out laughing, surprising herself and her friends. "You know what? I'm glad it wasn't the Batsquatch, too." She followed everyone into the dining room.

They had a nice, relaxing meal. Their conversation, stilted at first, soon became familiar as they chatted about when Autumn would return to her job and the challenges of Nate and Mike's positions. Tiffany worked for temp agencies and shared a couple of silly stories from a recent data entry job.

It seemed they silently agreed to table the Bigfoot talk until they were alone.

When they returned to their cabin, Autumn sank onto the couch. Zach had left another voice mail, expressing concern and sympathy for whatever had happened and letting her know he loved her. She would call him right after she got home tomorrow, hopefully able to finally directly connect with him again.

"Okay," Nate said. "Evidence dump. Mike, let's see what you have."

Mike connected his phone to the laptop and pulled up the photos. There were several that showed nothing but forest. The photos of the structure were good, and the pictures that Autumn had taken of the bones and the clothes were compelling. They looked at the pictures from the clearing, where Bigfoot was slightly out of focus. The next pictures that Mike had been able to take were from Autumn's attack, when he had been behind the Bigfoot. They could see the full outline of the creature, including the details of the hair color and length of its arms. There was only one good shot of the Bigfoot, and the rest were blurry as Mike had become more concerned about Autumn and turned off the camera.

"Your video, Autumn?" Nate asked. She connected her phone and pulled up the video. It started off smoothly, with the movement in the bushes visible and the appearance of a large animal near the tree. Once Autumn's hands started shaking, though, the video became almost useless.

"Damn," she said, disconnecting her phone. "At least we have the hair and bite samples. We can send that to a lab at some point."

"We had a near-perfect cast of that track," Mike reminded her. "I hope Ranger Tyler follows up on it and doesn't destroy it."

"What about those roars?" Tiffany asked. "Did you get any sounds other than the one from the video?"

"Oh, no," Nate said, suddenly realizing it. "We weren't recording."

They sat quietly for a moment. "You know, that's not a big deal," Mike said. "We have those pictures, we have most of Autumn's video, and we know what we saw. That's plenty to share with the forum and see what people have to say."

"I agree," Autumn said. "And I have pictures to add to the book."

"I think this was a success," Nate said. He looked at Autumn and his voice choked up. "Although we almost lost a friend."

She squeezed his hand. "I'm still here, and grateful for everyone's actions."

"Do you think we'll be able to sleep tonight?" Mike asked.

"I hope so," Autumn said. "But I'm not ready for bed yet. Why don't we sit outside and enjoy the fresh air? It's a nice night."

"Fire pit!" Tiffany exclaimed. "I'll go get some wood and matches."

"I'll get some blankets and the s'mores supplies," Mike said.

"I'll bring out some drinks," Nate promised.

"I'll just go sit outside," Autumn laughed. "That's all there's left to do."

They spent the next few hours out in the cool evening breeze, enjoying snacks, keeping the fire going, and laughing. Jenna and Donnie came along to let them know what time they needed to check out the next morning.

"I hope nothing goes bump in the night," Donnie said as he left. Jenna had clearly told him about Autumn's assertion that she had been attacked by a Bigfoot.

"I think we'll be left alone tonight," Autumn said. She smiled and watched the moonlight on the lake. She was alive and with her friends, and had experienced another successful Bigfoot hunt. She felt calm and at peace, and was looking forward to going home tomorrow.

Jake Tyler pulled into his driveway and once again waved at

Faye. This time she held up a hand, motioning for him to wait for her. He paused in front of his truck as his neighbor emerged from her front door. She held a flashlight in her hand, and had turned on the lights that illuminated the ground along all four sides of her house.

"Hi, Jake. How was your day?"

"Eventful," he responded honestly. "I don't think that whatever creature all of you think is in the forest will be here tonight."

"You're wrong," Faye said.

"What do you mean?" Jake asked. After Autumn and her friends had left, he had spent several hours talking to his boss and convincing him that yes, he was sure that he had only fired his weapon once, and that the animal he had hit was still alive. He had told the boss a bear had gotten into to the research area and that he had scared it off. He hoped that everyone who read the report believed him.

"Look, I know you don't believe that there's a Bigfoot around here. It's been seen throughout the park, but none of you rangers acknowledge it. You always tell us we're seeing a bear."

"Excuse me. You were the one who told me that you all saw a bear back there at the Bobcat Lake Project. I'm just passing that on to protect what I now know is really there."

Faye drew a sharp breath. "You saw Bigfoot?"

"Yes. I had to go rescue Autumn and her friends."

"I warned them last night to stay away from Bigfoot Ridge." Jake had to smile at Faye's easy use of the new name for the area. "I guess they didn't listen."

"No, they didn't. And to get back to your earlier point, most people new to hiking and camping do see bears doing something they're not expecting to see and start thinking they're seeing Bigfoot."

"Whatever." Faye waved that off. "Come here. There's something you should see."

"What is it?"

"Just take a look, Jake."

Jake reluctantly followed Faye around to the back of her house. She pointed at one of her back windows, which looked into the bathroom. "Last night, there was something looking in this window. I saw it when I started walking down the hall to the bathroom. It had a long snout and yellow eyes. When it saw me, it dropped out of sight."

"Long snout and yellow eyes?" His mind instantly went to a bear, but they had darker eyes. He opened his mouth.

She held up a hand. "Don't say it, Jake. Does a bear leave wolf tracks?"

"Wolf tracks?" he repeated numbly.

"Yes, wolf tracks. Large ones." She pointed down with the flashlight at an impression in the mud that was already clearly seen with the lights.

Jake kneeled down next to it. Faye was right. There were no wolves in Olympic National Park, and yet there was a wolf print right next to his knee. A very large wolf print. He stood up and shook his head. There was something in the report of his father's death that suddenly flashed into his mind, something about the wounds on the body and tracks around it that had led to the assumption of a bear attack.

John and Beth's story echoed in his brain. Autumn's assertion of a dogman in the park also popped into his head and he tried to get rid of the image. "All I can do is take some pictures and file this as a wild animal sighting," he told her.

She sighed. "I know, Jake. You don't need to do that. I just thought I'd show you in case you see something like this around your own house. Other people at the end of the road have noticed it, too."

Jake's heart sank. "Thanks, Faye." He took some pictures with his phone and made sure that Faye made it into her house. He locked his front door and turned on the porch light, then pulled all the shades on the windows. He microwaved his dinner and ate it, then sat down in front of the fireplace.

Seeing Bigfoot today had been a shock. He wondered how Autumn and her friends had seemed to remain so calm, then reasoned that it was possible they had seen the creature in another place. He went to his computer and pulled up the BOG website and ran a search for Autumn's name. The results included several trip reports and claims of having encountered both Bigfoot and the creature called a dogman near Mount Rainier.

An internet search of the dogman led him to sites mostly focused on sightings in Wisconsin and Michigan. He had to admit that such a creature could easily hide here in Olympic National Park. Any animals it killed could be attributed to another carnivore, and if it stayed silent instead of howling, people might not even suspect anything unless they happened to see it for themselves.

He shook his head and stood up. On his way to the kitchen to get a beer, he noticed that he had not pulled the shade on the back door. He looked out and noticed something standing down by the shore of the lake. It was tall and muscular, but slightly shorter and thinner than the Bigfoot he had seen today. It turned its head and he noticed the profile of a dog's head, with a long snout and upright ears. It took a few steps on its hind legs, then bent down to the water and scooped up water in what appeared to be a large paw.

"Dogman?" Jake said numbly, the new term immediately returning to his head. He pulled the shade and backed away. He hadn't seen any monsters in his life until today. He hoped this was the last time he would see them, but he had a feeling that as more people became interested in looking for these creatures, he'd be facing them during the course of his job. He returned to his chair in front of the fire, lost in thought, pondering the existence of monsters.

CHAPTER 18

On Tuesday morning, Autumn and her friends packed up and made sure the cabin was clean before heading to the parking lot with their gear. They checked out at the front desk and ate breakfast before saying goodbye to Jenna and Donnie. "We'll keep an eye out for strange creatures," Jenna assured them. "And we'll make sure Cole's not setting up any more hoaxes here."

Tiffany left first, and Mike drove away with the promise to call Nate when he got home. Nate helped Autumn with her luggage and got in the driver's seat. She felt odd being the passenger in her own car, but she got used to it as they drove along Bobcat Lake and finally left the park behind. On the way home, she pointed out the rest stop where she had her encounter on the way to the resort.

Nate pulled over to get a quick break, and Autumn walked to the grassy area where she had left the apples. They were all gone, but when she moved aside several ferns, she saw the rotting cores of the eaten apples. She backed away and smiled. Whatever animal had consumed the fruit, she hoped it had enjoyed them. They got back into the car and drove to Tacoma.

Tiffany was waiting for them, and Mike called just as Nate was getting out of Autumn's car. Nate helped Autumn into the house. "You're going to be okay?" he asked.

She nodded. Squatch came over to smell her the same way he always did when she was away for a few days. "Yes. Thank you."

"Take care of yourself." He and Tiffany both hugged her, and she waved to them from her front porch.

When Autumn returned to her living room, finally alone, she passed her suitcase in the foyer and headed straight to her favorite spot on the couch. Squatch stared at her. He seemed apprehensive about approaching her, especially with the sling on her arm, but when she patted the cushion next to her, he jumped up and started purring.

"We've got something," she told him. Her voice sounded tired in the otherwise silent room. "Maybe not all the solid proof we're always seeking. But it's a clear photo of a large, humanoid animal, and I can't wait to see what the people on the forum have to say about it."

She took out her phone and dialed Zach's number. "Hello?" he answered cheerfully. "How was your trip?"

"You're not going to believe what I have to tell you," Autumn said. "We had large rocks thrown at us, we have at least one good picture of Bigfoot, and I was almost killed."

He was silent for a moment. "Killed?" he asked weakly.

She explained that they had been doing call blasts when the creature appeared, and the ensuing chase that followed when the creature blocked their path. "The park ranger showed up in time to shoot the creature. That allowed us to get away."

"Shoot it? Did he kill it?"

"It was wounded when we last saw it, bleeding from its hands. I think he saw the same thing I did in its eyes. It was almost like some part of it was human, or had human feelings and emotions."

"What about the photo?" he asked. "Only one good one?"

She knew he must be thinking about her previous encounters with the creature, where there had been no doubt about what she had seen and touched. "Mike got it from the back while it was standing over me. We also got other pictures that are blurry, and some shaky video."

"I'm looking forward to seeing that picture," he told her. "Send it to me when you can."

"I will. I'm home now. Where are you?"

"In Kentucky," he said. "Revisiting the site of the Pope Lick Monster."

"Oh, Zach," she said, and covered her mouth. Her eyes filled with tears, but she wiped them away. Zach had encountered problems on his last visit to the infamous train trestle where the Pope Lick monster was rumored to lure his victims to their death.

"I'm okay," he assured her. "Brandon will be with me tonight when we explore around the trestle."

"You're not going out on the tracks, are you?" she asked.

"Not out on the trestle," he said. "We're staying well away from that."

"Are you hoping to see another goatman?"

"I'm still trying to understand my last encounter with one," he said, referencing his trip to Oregon earlier in the year. "From here we're going to Florida for a few weeks, then ending up in Missouri in early November."

"Missouri?" she asked. "What's there?"

"A rash of black-eyed kid sightings," he said. "I'm glad you're safe, Autumn. How are your friends?"

They chatted for a few more moments, then Zach had to leave. "I'll call you tomorrow," he promised. "Love you."

"Love you, too," she said. He hung up, and she headed straight to the computer to check out the post Mike had already written made about their trip. She scanned the first comment under the photo and write-up, which was from Cole Patterson.

"Looks like Bigfoot Ridge is the perfect name."

She smiled. Despite Cole's hoax, she knew that he was serious about cryptids and their discovery, leading to science finally recognizing creatures everyone now considered monsters. It was one reason why he interviewed people and shared stories that were sent to him. She decided to order a few of his books later in the week.

She saw there was another update to the Bigfoot track post from Friday. This time, a photo was attached of what appeared, from one angle, to be a large person climbing up the rocky cliff at the edge of Bigfoot Ridge. Another angle, taken from the side, revealed an outline that vaguely resembled a wolf. She smiled. Jake might have to accept evidence like this if he was still skeptical about a dogman. The comments in the post showed a lot of doubt about the creature, claiming that it was probably someone in a dog costume climbing the cliff for social media views. She had to admit that such a stunt was not impossible these days.

She received an e-mail and saw that it was from Nate. "Camera at the window caught something in the forest behind the cabin while we were at the clinic," she read. A file was attached, and she opened it with curiosity.

She could see the view from the loft window. No one appeared to be behind their cabin or passing by on the lake path. She could clearly see the start of the trail that led back to the nearest viewing tower. The time stamp indeed marked the video as being mid-afternoon on Monday.

Suddenly, tree limbs near the trail started shaking, just a few feet off the ground. She sat back in her chair and watched in fascination as the body of what appeared to be bipedal wolf appeared on the trail. It turned its head, leaving no doubt that this was indeed a dogman.

The creature turned its head and sniffed the air. It turned around, seemingly startled by something. The long fingers attached to large paws flexed in the air, and it slipped in between the trees. Autumn waited, then saw a deer emerging from the forest. It suddenly got dragged back into the bushes, and the shaking leaves indicated a struggle. Then, quiet returned to the area. The creature had found its next meal.

Autumn sat back. She had told Ranger Tyler about the dogman. She wondered what he'd tell any hikers if they described such a creature to him. He'd probably pass it off as a large coyote.

She called Nate. "Hey, did you see Cole's comment under our report?"

"Not yet."

She read it to him. "What do you think about posting your video?"

"Let's wait a bit. It might look like we're making one or the other up if we post both Bigfoot and dogman sightings from the same weekend around the same place."

"Yeah, you're right."

"How are you?"

"Tired. How's Tiffany?"

"Her ankle's feeling better. She actually asked when we were going to do it again."

"Good. Both of you should get some rest. Someday soon we'll all be back out on the trail."

Her work done for the day, she went upstairs and unpacked, took a shower, and returned to the first floor to start a load of laundry. It was slow going with her injured arm, but the process allowed her to unwind. Squatch followed her around the house, not wanting to let her out of his sight. When she had ordered dinner and returned to the computer to wait for her meal, she was satisfied with what she was reading.

Many people had responded to Mike's post, both for and against the possibility of what they saw really being Bigfoot. He had also included a photo of the footprint cast, which drew a large number of positive comments. Several people even urged him to follow up with the park service to see what they did with the track.

She turned off the computer. She closed her eyes and briefly thought back to the moment when she had been on her back, thinking that Bigfoot was about to kill her. She had been terrified, but in the aftermath of the event excitement had run through her body. She felt they had documented Bigfoot Ridge as well as they could, and there was no need to go back.

She was intrigued by the dogman footage, though. That might be worth another exploration in the Olympic National Park. She would definitely keep an eye out for any reports on that cryptid in the area.

She ate her dinner, then sat back down on the couch. A quick scan at the television channel guide showed re-runs of *Creature Hunt* on for the rest of the evening. She changed the channel and sat back to watch Zach on the lookout for the dogman in Michigan.

"Keep going, Zach," she said out loud. "We're going to show these creatures to the world."

ABOUT THE AUTHOR

C.E. Osborn grew up in Tacoma, Washington, and currently resides in New Jersey. She is a cataloging librarian and enjoys reading mysteries and stories about cryptid creatures. You can learn more at www.ceosborn.wordpress.com and on Facebook.

Works by C.E. Osborn

Bigfoot Ridge
Tahoma Valley
Days of Halloween
Trail of Monsters
Wolf Crossing
October Nights
Creature Hunt
Circle of Darkness
Shadow in the Trees
Camp Thunder Cloud

Poetry:
Dream Softly
Before You Take My Hand

Lonely Hollow series:

Haunted Hollow
Secret Hollow
Stormy Hollow
Winter Hollow
Lonely Hollow